"Whoops!"

With a resounding crash, the magic mirror landed on the floor and broke into a thousand pieces.

"Oh, I'm so sorry," Sabrina said. "What am I going to do?"

"That's what I was just about to ask you myself," the Quizmaster said as he appeared in her doorway. "What *are* you going to do?"

"Quizmaster, please," Sabrina begged. "This is not a good time."

Her magic tutor laughed. "You're telling me. You broke a magic mirror. Do you know what that means? For breaking a magic mirror, you bring upon yourself seven—"

She winced. "Seven years of bad luck, I know."

"Days of bad luck," he finished at the same time.

She brightened. "Only one week?"

"Wait a minute. Don't get all happy on me. You're in for one tough week," the Quizmaster said. "Mortals get seven years of bad luck because they don't have any magic powers. But you'll get more in seven days than they could handle in seven *lifetimes.*"

Sabrina, the Teenage Witch™ books

Available from Archway Paperbacks

Sabrina ★ The Teenage Witch™

Eight Spells a Week

SUPER EDITION

Based on Characters Appearing in Archie Comics

**And based upon the television series
Sabrina, The Teenage Witch
Created for television by Nell Scovell
Developed for television by Jonathan Schmock**

AN ARCHWAY PAPERBACK
Published by POCKET BOOKS
New York London Toronto Sydney Tokyo Singapore

AN ARCHWAY PAPERBACK *Original*

An Archway Paperback published by
POCKET BOOKS, a division of Simon & Schuster Inc.
1230 Avenue of the Americas, New York, NY 10020

ISBN: 0-671-02121-4

First Archway Paperback printing January 1999

10 9 8 7 6 5 4 3 2

Printed in the U.S.A.

IL: 4+

Calendar

Calendar

Eight Spells
a Week

SUNDAY

The Mirror Crack'd Up
By Nancy Holder

At the tone the time will be . . . even later than you think," Salem drawled as Sabrina rushed madly around the kitchen. The black cat was sitting on the counter beside the toaster, and his head made little circles as he watched Sabrina Spellman dart from place to place.

"Salem, I know I'm on the downside of being ready on time," Sabrina gritted, "but it doesn't help when you nudge me." She pointed at the oven and the scent of freshly baked chocolate chip cookies filled the air.

Salem shrugged. "Just trying to help. Mmm, those smell good enough to eat. Hint, hint."

"No. You can't have any," Sabrina ordered him. "These are for the tea."

"Ah, the tea. Who are you taking, Hilda or Zelda?"

"Aunt Zelda. Aunt Hilda's sequestered for

3

Witches' Council duty. I can't even talk to her, much less invite her anywhere." Sabrina hurried over to the refrigerator and pointed open the door. "Where's my lemonade?"

"Your what?"

"Salem, I made a gallon of lemonade!" She whirled around and glared at him in exasperation. *"Please,* don't tell me you drank all of it."

"I won't." He burped. "Whoops, excuse me."

She squinted at him. "I smell lemons, cat."

"It's your imagination," he assured her. Then he yawned. "And frankly, all this . . . activity is wearing me out. I think I'll take a nap." So saying, he flopped over on his side, closed his eyes, and began to snore.

"Oooh, you!" Sabrina muttered, pointing at him. Then she pulled back her finger as he began to snore again. As a rule, she tried not to use magic on Salem. For one thing, it didn't seem right, since as a warlock-turned-cat, he couldn't use any himself. And for another, except for the occasional sarcastic remark and the disgusting tendency to hack up fur balls in her closet, he was a pretty good cat.

But truth be told, all this activity was wearing her out, too. She had a million things to do before the Westbridge High's annual Mother-Daughter/Primary-Caregiver/Court-Appointed-Guardian/Parole-Officer/Big-Sister tea. Not only was she supposed to bring a tray of food and something to drink, but she was supposed to bring a mother.

And her mother was in Peru on an archeology dig.

Not a problem for a witch? Or even a half-witch? All she had to do was point her mom here and they could go to the tea, right?

Wrong. So very, very wrong.

Sabrina's mother was a mortal. Her father, a warlock. Making Sabrina the product of a "mixed" mortal-witch marriage. And as such marriages were discouraged by the Witches' Council, if Sabrina saw her mother any time before she turned eighteen—for even one second—her mother would be turned into a ball of wax. Forever.

"So scratch one mom," Sabrina grumbled. As usual, one of her full-witch aunts, Hilda or Zelda, would accompany her to the school function. Sabrina lived with her aunts so that they could teach her how to use her powers.

And as usual, Libby Chessler would take it upon herself to make some pointed comment about Sabrina's missing mother.

"We should have told everyone she's a spy or something," Sabrina said under her breath, then shook her head. She couldn't exactly lie about her mother's whereabouts. And she really *was* on a dig in Peru, which is what Sabrina had told her friends when she had moved here.

But as Libby loved to observe, it did seem strange that not once, in all that time, not for

Christmas, or a birthday, or school vacation, had Sabrina's mother come to visit her.

"I guess she doesn't think you're very important," Libby had once said, sniffing. And that had cut Sabrina to the quick. Because what could she say? It certainly did appear that way, didn't it? And there was nothing Sabrina could say to prove otherwise.

"Not that it matters," she murmured.

The phone rang. Sabrina pointed it to her ear.

"Sabrina, you will not believe this!" It was Valerie, her best friend. "My mom bought us matching mother-daughter dresses."

"Oh, cool," Sabrina said, trying to hide her envy.

"Cool? Are you crazy? That might have been cool when I was in kindergarten, but not high school! Everyone's going to laugh at us."

"I won't," Sabrina promised her. "What do they look like?"

"Oh." Sabrina could practically hear Valerie rolling her eyes. "Frilly. Incredibly frilly. Our ruffles have ruffles. I look like pink whipped cream."

"Your mom has good taste," Sabrina offered, then giggled. "In clothes *and* dessert toppings. I'm sure you look just great."

"Well, this will certainly put our friendship to the test," Valerie said dryly. "Because if you'll still be seen with me while I'm wearing this, then I'll know I can count on you in any crisis. Because I didn't tell you about the matching shoes yet. Or the hat."

Sabrina's eyes widened. "The *hat?*"

"The hat." Valerie sighed. "You have no idea."

"I guess I don't." Sabrina shrugged. "But it'll be so neat to have your mom there and all."

"Yeah, I guess." Valerie sounded resigned. "Are your aunts coming?"

Suddenly Sabrina smelled smoke. She whirled around and saw smoke pouring out of the oven.

"My cookies!" she cried. "Val, gotta go!"

"See you there," Valerie said, as Sabrina hung up.

Sabrina raced to the oven and pointed it open. Huge clouds of smoke roiled from the cookie sheet, on which sat sixteen charred cinders.

"What? What?" Salem shouted, coming awake. "The enemy is attacking!"

Sabrina pointed the cookie sheet to the cooling rack on the opposite side of the sink and groaned. "Salem, it's not the enemy, it's my cookies. Look at them!"

"Oh, I was having nightmares again," Salem said, wrinkling his nose, "about the time when I was just about to complete my plan for world domination, when all of a sudden, they set the fort on fire."

"You were never in a fort," Sabrina said, picking him up and carrying him from the kitchen.

"However, you were stopped, and now you're a cat."

"And now you have nothing to take to the tea," Salem said helpfully.

"I know. I know," Sabrina said. She pointed open some windows and carried Salem upstairs out of the smoke-filled kitchen.

"What are you doing?" he demanded.

"Valerie's call reminded me that I have to figure out what to wear," she said. "Then I'll try to cook something else the old-fashioned way." She huffed down the hall and into her room. Setting Salem on her bed, she said, "You weigh a ton."

"It's all that lemonade . . . um, Pretty Kitty cat food," he said quickly. "I keep asking for Pretty Kitty Lite, but you people never listen."

"Uh-huh." Sabrina wasn't really listening. Her face fell as she pointed open her closet. "But what am I supposed to wear?"

"Whatever people wear to a Boston tea party," Salem said.

Right! Sabrina pointed at herself and said:

"That Salem, he's a smarty!
For clothes, let's go Boston tea party."

Whoosh!

She was standing on the deck of a sailing ship. Around her, some men dressed in Indian deer-skins hurled crates over the side of the ship. One shouted, "No taxation without representation! No tax on tea!"

Salem bobbed his head up from a barrel. He was wearing a three-corner hat on top of a white wig. To Sabrina he said, "Betsy Ross, I presume?"

"What?" She looked down at herself. She was wearing a white ruffled blouse and a flounced skirt.

"Salem," she said, finally putting two and two together. "This is 1773. We're at *the* Boston Tea Party, when the colonists threw imported British tea overboard!"

"I know. Isn't it fun?" A tea bag dangled by its string from Salem's mouth. With a jaunty toss of his head, it sailed into the water. The others cheered his defiant act.

"Yes, but I'm not showing up at *my* tea dressed like this."

Sabrina pointed and chanted:

"Back to Westbridge, toil and trouble,
To the present, on the double!"

Whoosh!

They were back in Westbridge.

"Well! That's more like it," Sabrina said. She hurried to her closet. "But I still don't know what to wear."

"I would think that's the least of your troubles," Salem pointed out.

"See, that's why you're a cat, and I'm a girl."

9

She was going through everything in her closet, pointing to it, suspending it in the air as she considered it, then pointing it to flop onto her bed beside Salem.

"Mmm, this is going to be one soft napping spot," Salem murmured to himself.

"Salem," she said anxiously, "what *am* I going to wear?"

"Ya know, if you ask me, which I realize you have not, but you should, I would go with the white shirt and the green pants," said a voice Sabrina didn't recognize. "Most definitely."

"Salem?" she asked, peering down at the cat.

He shook his head. "That wasn't me. I would never suggest that outfit."

Sabrina looked around. "Who's in here?"

"Hey, girlie, it's me. Over here."

Sabrina crept forward.

"You're getting warmer."

She moved to the right, near the door to her room.

"Colder."

She moved to the left, in the direction of her bay window.

"Warmer."

"Hey." She brightened. Sitting in the bay window, among her pillows and stuffed animals, gleamed a medium-sized oval mirror in an ornate gold frame. A bow was jauntily attached to one corner, along with a note. Sabrina picked it up.

"Hey, yourself, girlie." The mirror's surface

showed the face of a woman with lots of heavy blue eye shadow and big blond hair bubbled into place with a turquoise jeweled headband. The face winked at her and smiled. "How's tricks, toots?"

"You're a magic mirror," Sabrina said, setting it on her bed and reaching for the note.

"Right you are. The very one, in fact, that Snow White's evil stepmother used to ask who was the fairest in the land. *Oy.* Talk about your dysfunctional family."

"What are you doing in our house?" Sabrina asked, admiring herself in it. "And, um, who *is* the fairest—"

"Don't start with me," the mirror chastised her. "Your aunts found me at a garage sale. Some mortal had gotten hold of me. Don't even make me tell you how. It's a very long and boring story. Also, somewhat embarrassing."

"But why would anyone sell a magic mirror?"

The mirror wrinkled her nose. "Well, let me tell you. Those mortals had no fashion sense. They'd look in me and just smile and pose like they were going to be listed in the *Evil Stepmothers' Who's Who.* It was terrible. Big, bold prints on the short ones, vertical stripes on the boy, who was as tall as Kareem—"

"So they sold you because they got tired of listening to you?" Sabrina cut in.

"No, no. They couldn't hear me at all. Couldn't see me, either. Oh, didn't I mention it? Only witches can see or hear me." The mirror winked. "You're a half witch. I can tell these things. I got the nose for it. You must be good, to be able to find me in the glass."

"Really?" Sabrina was thrilled. "Well, that's great." She glanced down at the note:

Dear Sabrina,
You're the fairest in our land! We love you. Enjoy.

Aunt Hilda and Aunt Zelda

"They're so sweet. I'll have to remember to thank them both. Hilda's supposed to be back from Council duty on Monday."

She reached behind herself. "So, the white and green?"

The mirror closed her eyes and nodded. "Trust me."

"No, no, no," Salem protested. "It's all wrong for the tea. Trust *me.*"

"Oh, you're going to a tea party?" the mirror asked. "Sorry, I misunderstood. I thought you were going to a golf tournament. *Tee*ing off and all that, don'tcha know." She studied Sabrina for a moment. "Blue dresses and white pinafores do wonders for blondes. Alice always looked great at the Wonderland tea parties."

"You used to belong to Alice in Wonderland?" Sabrina asked, delighted.

"Naw, the Queen of Hearts. Maybe you should consider a nice pastel. You're so fair and all. Maybe some little gloves and a matching hat."

"Oh, puh-lese," Salem said.

"What's wrong with that?" the mirror demanded. "At least give it a try."

Sabrina shrugged. "What the hey." She pointed to herself and poof!

Ouch! A quick glance in the mirror told her she looked almost exactly like Alice, except with little white gloves and a straw hat with bunches of ribbons that reached to her shoulders. It looked like a balloon hat from a little kid's birthday party.

"Hmm, on you it's not so right," the mirror said. "Let me think . . ."

"You still have another batch of cookies to bake," Salem suggested. "And in the next batch of lemonade, add more sugar."

"Dear girl, why don't you run downstairs and attend to all that," the mirror suggested, "and I'll think about your ensemble."

"My ensemble," Sabrina said under her breath. "Sure."

She ran downstairs and threw a spell for finger sandwiches together. A tray appeared with long, thin sandwiches arranged in neat little rows. Then she murmured something she hoped made sense about iced tea. A pitcher magically appeared beside the sandwiches.

"Yes!" she cried, and turned to go . . . just as the sandwiches started waving at her. Then one flopped on its side while the one beside it stood up on one end. The next two bent over double, and the fifth one also stood up. She stared at them for a moment. Then she got it: The fingers were forming the American Sign Language sign for "I love you!"

"You love me? Then how can I let anyone eat you?" she asked in dismay.

"Oy, mein girlie, I've got something really stunning up here for you!" the mirror called from upstairs.

"Oh, okay," Sabrina called back anxiously. To the finger sandwiches, she said, "I'll be right back."

She turned and started running up the stairs. But she had the distinct feeling she was being followed. She whirled around and saw a miniature parade of sandwiches trailing behind her.

"My fingers are doing the walking!" she wailed. She pointed at them. "Stay!"

The clock in the living room bonged 3:00 P.M. Aunt Zelda was due home in a few minutes, and they had to leave for the tea by 3:15. What was she going to do?

"Mirror?" she called, zooming into her room, just as Salem jumped down from the bed. "Whoops!"

Sabrina made a little leap over him, realized she

couldn't stop her momentum, sailed in an arc toward her bed—and almost landed on the mirror. To avoid it, she pushed at it with her hand, sending it cascading over the edge of her bed.

With a resounding crash, it landed on the floor and broke into a thousand pieces.

"Oh, no!" Sabrina cried, scooting across the bed to inspect the damage.

The mirror frame was completely empty. Shards of rainbow-sparkling glass glittered on the floor.

In one piece, larger than the others, the blue-tinted eyelid of the mirror's face opened slowly and stared up at Sabrina.

"Oh, I'm so sorry," she said. "What am I going to do?"

Almost as fast as she had broken the mirror, Sabrina jumped off the bed in surprise at the sight of her Quizmaster, standing in her doorway.

"That's what I was just about to ask you myself," he said. "What *are* you going to do?"

"Quizmaster, please," Sabrina begged. "This is not a good time."

Her magic tutor laughed. "You're telling me. You broke a magic mirror. Do you know what that means?"

"Um, no more fashion tips?" she ventured.

He shrugged. "No, you can still get those. Trust me, you don't want to wear the white and green."

"Good man," Salem said, licking his paw. "For

those who are concerned, no, I didn't step on any of the broken glass. And thanks so much for asking."

The Quizmaster shook his head. "Sabrina, Sabrina, Sabrina."

"Quizmaster, Quizmaster, Quizmaster," she said anxiously.

"For breaking a magic mirror, you bring upon yourself seven—"

She winced. "Seven years of bad luck, I know."

"Days of bad luck," he finished at the same time.

She brightened. "Only one week?"

"Wait a minute. Don't get all happy on me. You are in for one tough week," the Quizmaster said. "Mortals get seven years of bad luck because they don't have any magic powers. But you'll get more in seven days more than they could handle in seven *lifetimes.*"

"Oy, vey," Sabrina groaned. "And you always wonder why I'm never very thrilled to see you. Well, thanks for the warning. But, um, I have a million things to do and—"

"Now, listen. This is serious stuff. It just so happens that there are Seven Temptations of Witchcraft." He smiled. "One for every day of the week as well."

Sabrina frowned at him. "You can't do this to me the same week as my week of bad luck."

He rubbed his hands together eagerly. "See, it really dovetails very nicely. Each day, you'll receive a stroke of bad luck that you'll be tempted to fix in a way you're not allowed to fix it. So, you'll have all these challenges, see, and when you overcome them—"

The light dawned. "You'll have something to brag about at next year's Quizmaster Luncheon?"

"Well, yes, that's true," he allowed. "But I'm doing it for your own good."

"You're so thoughtful," she said.

"And clever." He winked at her. "Don't worry, Sabrina. I'm sure you're going to come through this with flying colors. Which, in America, are red, white, and blue, I might add."

With that he disappeared.

"Thanks for the vote of confidence," Sabrina said.

Coming up beside her, Salem burped.

The phone rang. It was Valerie. "We're leaving a little early," she said anxiously, "so we can pick up our matching corsages. Please, meet me there. No one else is going to talk to me dressed like this. I'm going to just die!"

"Oh." Sabrina bit her lower lip. "Valerie, I'm running a little late."

"No, you can't be late! Don't make me stand around dying a thousand deaths all by myself."

"Okay." Sabrina grimaced. "Then I gotta go, okay?"

She pointed the phone back to its base. "Oh, great," she muttered. "What am I going to do?"

"Check on the sandwiches," Salem said, "before I do."

"Oh, you talk big, but you'd never eat them," Sabrina said. He gave her a coy kitty meow and she added anxiously, "Would you?"

"No, I wouldn't, and teasing you is beginning to lose its appeal. Just go down there and zap something up. Your aunts do it all the time."

"Okay, okay."

She dashed around the corner and started back down the stairs, where the sandwiches were doing the wave.

"Excuse me, excuse me," she said, darting around them.

As she ran into the kitchen, the toaster popped. Sabrina hurried to it. They often received correspondence from the Other Realm via the toaster.

> *Dear Sabrina,*
> *I'm so sorry, but I've been summoned before the Committee for Mortal Involvement to defend my participation in a mortal physics think tank. I won't be able to go to the tea, dear.*
> *I should come out of this without a reprimand. After all, I have contributed greatly to the advancement of science. Wish me luck!*
> *Your loving Aunt Zelda*

"You don't want my luck," Sabrina said.

"Bad news?" Salem asked, sauntering into the

kitchen. Two sandwiches were merrily riding his back. "Already?"

"Aunt Zelda can't go to the tea," Sabrina wailed. "Oh, Salem, I have to be able to take a primary caregiver. Everyone's taking a primary caregiver."

"Actually, it's my understanding that most of them are taking their mothers." Salem turned his head and said to one of the sandwiches, "Can you scratch a little lower? Ahh, very nice."

"What's a think tank?" Sabrina asked, rereading the note.

"It's like a fish tank, only smarter," Salem told her.

She sighed. "Okay, I need to figure out what to do." She brightened. "I could make a mom out of Mom Dough."

"We're out," Salem said. He made a face. "Hey, I got lonesome for *my* mom last Christmas. To tell you the truth, though, it didn't work out very well."

"And Libby's going to be watching me like a hawk," Sabrina mused. "Which is also why I better not invite Great Grandma."

She turned to the portrait of Aunt Louisa on the wall. "Would you like to go?"

The portrait sighed. "I'm sorry, honey, I'm just feeling kind of flat today."

"Okay," Sabrina said in a small voice.

"Maybe you should skip it," Salem suggested.

"That's tempting. Aha! That must be the First Temptation: to give up. To not use my powers to help myself, when I can help myself. So I have to go. Plus, I promised Valerie I'd be there." Sabrina thought for a moment. "You know, Salem, I *could* send my mom to the tea. I'm half-witch, after all!"

"There's that little ball of wax problem," Salem pointed out.

"But I'll just make sure I'm never in the same room with her." Sabrina nodded happily. "It won't be that hard. I can do it. I just need my magic book."

She ran back upstairs, Salem grumbling and huffing as the sandwiches, also tiring, all tried to leap on his back for a free ride.

Sabrina pointed the pieces of broken mirror into a box, then hurried over to her book and flipped it open. Which spell to try? First she looked at Conjuring Mortals. No, that probably meant conjuring up someone out of thin air. All she wanted was to . . . Transport!

"Yes." She read the directions to herself. "Let's see. I need a cup of jet stream and some fairy dust. Cool!" She continued down the list. "Uh-oh, something near and dear to the traveler in question."

She started looking around her desk. "What's something that's near and dear to my mom?"

Then she caught her reflection in one of the shards.

"Me!" she cried. "I'm near and dear to my mom."

"Sniff." She turned to see Salem all teary. "I miss my mom, too."

"We can transport her, too," Sabrina said eagerly.

"No, you try it on your mother first. If it doesn't work . . ."

"Salem, what's not to work?" she asked cheerily.

Moving fast, Sabrina gathered the ingredients together. There was some fairy dust in the pantry. She was a little anxious to take the vacuum cleaner out for a spin to collect the jet stream in broad daylight, so she sent up a couple of very obliging finger sandwiches in a teacup tied to a helium balloon.

While she waited for them to return, she found a lacy white tea dress with handkerchief sleeves and a matching hemline on her bed. It must have been the ensemble the mirror whipped up before Sabrina broke her.

"This is what I should have put on in the first place," she said, nodding.

Then she calmly pointed a tray of fruit and cheese into existence. Her iced tea turned out to be fine.

"See, if you just stay confident, you can do all kinds of things," she told Salem. "My big mistake was losing my cool in the first place."

But Salem had dozed off.

The finger sandwiches returned with the jet stream. Sabrina poured it into a cup of fairy dust and whirled it in a vortex around herself.

> *"Mother, mother in Peru,*
> *your witchly daughter summons you!*
> *To the tea go straight away,*
> *And from my sight, please stay away."*

Whoosh! The vortex rose up over Sabrina and flashed out through the ceiling. Sabrina took a breath and murmured, "I hope it worked. 'Bye, Salem! Gotta go!"

She tried a version of the Transport spell on herself and appeared in the girls' bathroom down the hall from the Westbridge High cafeteria, where the tea was being held.

Yes! In the center of the floor there was a little pile of sand, and in the center of it, a set of footprints. They looked the same size as her mother's. And there was a hand print, too—a little dusty—on a paper towel that hadn't made it to the trash bin. Sabrina set down her cheese and fruit tray and pitcher of iced tea, picked up the towel, and placed her hand over it. Yes. It had to be her mom's hand print.

"Woo hoo! She's here!" Sabrina cried, picked up her tray and pitcher, and ran out of the bathroom into the corridor. She heard the hum of voices and laughter and the clink of dishes.

Then she stopped. How was she going to make sure she never saw her mother?

Uncertainly, she took a step toward the cafeteria. Then the door opened and she caught her breath and closed her eyes, just in case.

"Sabrina! Finally!"

It was Valerie. Sabrina opened her eyes and almost burst out in a shocked guffaw. Poor Valerie looked like a float in the Rose Parade. Her fussy dress was a mass of floral ruffles and pink lace, and a corsage the size of a cabbage was drooping off the bodice. An enormous straw hat was covered with silk flowers—as well as matching ribbons and bows—that matched the dress. She looked like pink whipped cream covered with pink sparkles, pink chopped nuts, pink syrup. The corsage was the bright red cherry that topped it all off.

Luckily, Sabrina caught herself and said, "Hey. Um . . ."

"Oh, don't even start with me," Valerie said, sighing. "You should hear what Libby had to say." She smiled. "But your mom was really cool about it. She's great, Sabrina. Why didn't you tell me she was coming?"

"I . . . it was a surprise."

"I love her pith helmet. And those little boots are too cute," Valerie went on. "Well, I was going to run into the bathroom for a good cry, but since you're here, I'll wait for the next insulting remark Libby makes."

"Oh." Sabrina stared at the closed door. Her mother was already there, and Sabrina couldn't see her.

She wished she'd thought this through a little more.

"Uh, well, actually, I need to use the restroom, but I wanted to bring my stuff in first," Sabrina said, holding up her tray and pitcher. "Would you mind taking these in for me? I'll be there in a jiffy."

"Okay." Valerie took them. "I didn't really want to miss your mom's story about finding the hidden burial chamber, anyway. Of course, I'm sure you've heard it a million times already."

Valerie turned on her heel and hurried back into the cafeteria.

"No," Sabrina said weakly. "I've never heard that story."

She went back into the bathroom. She wasn't sure what to do. She had to make an appearance at the tea, but she didn't want to turn her mother into a ball of wax.

Footsteps sounded in the hall, followed by the voice of Mrs. Quick, saying, "Oh, Ms. Spellman, that's such a wonderful story!"

"Thank you." Sabrina's eyes widened. Her mother's voice was behind the bathroom door. *Uh-oh! They're coming in the bathroom!*

Sabrina tried the nearest door, which is where the janitor kept the cleaning supplies. It was locked! Sabrina pointed at it, but she was so freaked out she couldn't remember the spell to unlock it.

"She said she'd be in here," Valerie offered.

The door began to open. Sabrina darted into one of the stalls, climbed onto the lid of the toilet, and hunkered down. *Mom knows. She knows she can't see me.*

Her mother said again, "Sabrina?"

Sabrina swallowed hard. She wanted like anything to answer, but she dare not. Not with Val and Mrs. Quick hovering nearby.

This had not been her best idea.

"Well, I'll just freshen up," her mom said.

Sabrina tried to peer at her mother through the crack between the door and the rest of the stall. Sure enough, she saw her mother's hair and back. She was dressed in a mid-calf khaki dress with a very nice leather belt and matching heeled boots. It must be what archeologists wore on fancy occasions out on their digs.

Her mother bent to look at herself in the mirror above the sink. Sabrina darted out of sight, just in case any part of her was reflected over her mother's shoulder into the mirror.

"Have you seen any of the school, Ms. Spellman?" Mrs. Quick asked. "Sabrina's classrooms?"

"No. I was hoping someone . . . uh, *Sabrina* would show me around," her mother said.

"Maybe Sabrina went to get something out of

her locker," Valerie suggested. "If that's the case, we'll run into her and we can all look around together."

"That would be lovely, Valerie," Sabrina's mom said.

They left the bathroom. Sabrina waited a beat, then raced out herself, making a beeline for the cafeteria. She flung herself inside, then cleared her throat as heads turned in her direction.

She slowed down, smiled at no one in general, and headed for the refreshment table, which was covered with a lacy cloth that matched her dress. There was her fruit and cheese tray, and there was her iced tea.

And there was Libby, standing behind the table, pouring punch for some of the other mothers and daughters.

"Sabrina," she said sweetly, "your mother is fantastic! She's nothing like what I expected."

"Oh." Sabrina managed a weak smile in return. "What did you expect?"

"A freak. Like you." She handed a cup of tea to Valerie's mother, who was dressed exactly like Valerie. In fact, they could have been twins, down to the enormous corsage.

"Well, surprise, surprise," Sabrina murmured, picking up a ladle and serving herself some of her iced tea. "My mother's the coolest in the land." She put it to her lips and made a little face. It was very, very sweet. She wondered if a certain cat had helped her out by emptying the sugar bowl into it.

"She's so pretty. And so interesting." Libby cocked her head. "It's so hard to believe she's your mother."

"Oh, um, yeah," Sabrina said, swallowing down the insults as she basked in the compliments about her mother. Actually, this was working out better than she'd hoped. She'd always known Libby would be impressed with her mom. This appearance was certain to raise Sabrina's social standing.

"And here she is," Libby said, brightening. She waved a hand in greeting. "Hello again, Ms. Spellman."

"Yikes!" Sabrina dropped to her hands and knees. "Contact lens," she blurted, "I dropped my . . ." That wouldn't work. She didn't wear contact lenses, and Libby knew it. "Earring that *looks* like a contact lens," she amended. "Oh, dear. I think it rolled under the table."

She lifted the tablecloth and crawled beneath the table. *Now what?*

"Sabrina, what are you doing?" Libby demanded. "Ouch! That's my foot."

"Nice shoes," Sabrina muttered. "Just looking for something," she said brightly. Like a trap door.

Hey! Why don't I point one up?

She was just about to attempt it when someone clapped their hands, as if for attention. "Ladies,

27

girls, I have a wonderful announcement! Sabrina's mother has offered to show us slides of her dig in Peru."

"Here's the slide projector." That was Valerie.

"Oh, thank you, dear. And here's Jeanie with the screen," chirped Mrs. Quick.

There were the sounds of wheels and things being set up.

"Everyone have a seat? Good," Mrs. Quick said. "Libby, would you get the lights?"

"Of course."

The room went dark.

This was Sabrina's chance. Gingerly lifting up the tablecloth, she again saw her mother, standing with her back to her. Sabrina's eyes welled with tears. She wanted to see her, talk to her, and give her a big hug.

"Here's the dig itself," her mother was saying. She held a pointer to the illuminated shot on the screen. "See that shape? That's a mummy."

"Wow," everyone breathed. They were enthralled. Sabrina's mom was the hit of the tea.

Slowly, Sabrina crawled in the dark among the chairs. "Sorry," she whispered when she rested her knee on someone's shoe. "Earring."

"And here are the mummy's golden collar and crown," Sabrina's mom went on, to *oohs* and *aahs*.

Sabrina's hands and knees were very sore by the time she reached the door, pushed it open very slowly, and crawled over the threshold.

The door swung quietly shut behind her. Sabrina groaned and got to her feet.

On the other side of the door, there was intense applause, and then the scrape of chairs being moved. Apparently the slide show was over.

Sabrina had the feeling it was time to get out of Dodge and head for home. Fast!

Behind her the door flew open. Sabrina cried, "Yeek!" in a tiny voice and tried to dash forward.

"Sabrina, there you are!" Valerie cried. "I want to get a picture of you with your mother for the school paper. Come on."

"No, no," Sabrina protested. "Valerie—"

"Don't be shy," Valerie said, dragging her into the room.

"No, because—"

Sabrina saw her mother facing Mrs. Quick, whose smile lit up as she urged Valerie and Sabrina forward. Jeanie, who had brought in the projector screen, stood poised with a camera.

"Oh, yes, dear, come on over for a picture," Mrs. Quick said. "Your mother is just so fascinating!"

And at that moment, Sabrina's mother turned.

And saw Sabrina.

Sabrina saw her.

Her mother smiled.

Nothing happened to her.

Sabrina's mouth dropped open.

"Come on, sweetheart," her mother said, holding open both arms.

29

Numbly, Sabrina walked toward her, expecting at any instant to see her mother transform into a ball of wax . . . all because she, Sabrina, had been so selfish that she'd been willing to put her own mother in danger.

But the moment didn't come. They posed for several pictures. Then they were surrounded by the other mothers and daughters, who commented on how alike they were, how nice it was to finally meet Sabrina's mother, and so on.

"And Sabrina's my best friend," Valerie crowed, as Sabrina's mother put an arm over Valerie's shoulder. She murmured, "Wow, this makes up a lot for the hat and gloves."

Sabrina chuckled uncertainly.

Then it was time to go. Sabrina's mother walked with Sabrina into the girls' bathroom and said, "Shall we?"

And before Sabrina realized what was happening, she and her mother were popped back to her aunts' house.

"Hey," Sabrina said, as the vortex disappeared. "Mom, you can't do magic!"

"No, she can't. But I can!"

In place of her mother stood her third full-witch aunt, the glamourous, often eccentric Aunt Vesta, dressed in a shimmering evening gown and a diamond tiara. Vesta lived in the Other Realm in her Pleasuredome, and she popped by occasionally to visit her favorite niece.

Vesta laughed and quickly gave Sabrina a hug.

"Don't worry, honey. It was me all along!" she assured her dumbstruck niece.

"You pretended to be my mother?"

Vesta nodded. "Zelda contacted me about the tea as soon as she realized she was in trouble for meddling with mortal affairs. I don't understand why she bothers, but what can one do?"

She twirled in a circle. When she stopped, she looked exactly like Sabrina's mother, from her pith helmet to her leather boots. "You were running around like a maniac when I arrived here, and I was almost too late to intercept your Transport spell. But I did."

She wagged her finger at Sabrina. "And lucky thing, too. You know we're not all that fond of your mother—it's no secret—but I still didn't want to see her end up as a ball of wax." She narrowed her eyes at her niece. "And I'm sure you didn't, either."

Sabrina hung her head. "It was a stupid idea," she admitted. "It's just that—"

"You miss her very, very much," Vesta said simply, as she led the way upstairs. Salem and the finger sandwiches were all cuddled up asleep on Salem's soft pillow next the phone. "You wanted to show her off in front of your friends, just like any daughter who's proud of her mother. Believe me, honey, I understand."

"I thought if Libby saw her, it would like, impress her." She smiled faintly. "And it did."

"Yes, it did. I made sure of that." Vesta checked

her jeweled watch. "Well, it was so fun . . . well, sort of fun. Good heavens, why would anyone in their right mind spend their time mucking around in cobwebs and dirt?"

She patted Sabrina's cheek. "Well, I suppose it's a good thing that there are so many different people in the world. But I must fly, darling. I'm giving a party myself, in my Pleasuredome. Would you like to come?"

Sabrina shook her head as she opened the linen closet, which also served as the Spellmans' portal to the Other Realm. "Thanks, Aunt Vesta, but I've had enough excitement for one day."

Vesta gave her a kiss on each cheek. "All right then, dear. *Ciao!*"

She stepped into the closet and Sabrina shut the door. With a flash of light and the peal of thunder, Vesta left for the Other Realm.

Sabrina walked into her bedroom and bent over the box of broken mirror pieces.

Then *poof!* the Quizmaster appeared, standing beside Sabrina's desk. He was holding a tea cup.

"Oh, hi," Sabrina said uneasily. "Again."

"Hello," the Quizmaster said. He swirled the cup, looked into it, and showed it to Sabrina. There were wet tea leaves in the bottom.

"Reading my fortune?" she asked, trying to smile.

"Maybe. Let's see." He studied the clump of leaves. "This is what I read: It may appear that you've taken your lumps, but this next week won't be a tempest in a teapot. Trouble's brewing, and you'd better think about what you learned today."

"I did learn something," she said.

"And that is?" he asked enthusiastically. "To avoid the temptation to put mortals in danger for any reason whatsoever?"

"Uh, yeah. That's it."

"Good!" he clapped his hands. "One down, Sabrina."

He disappeared.

Yawning, Salem wandered into the room and jumped up to the bed. Some of the sandwiches did the same.

He said, "Passed the first part of your Bad Luck Week quiz, eh?"

Sabrina grimaced. "Actually, what I was going to tell my Quizmaster that I learned was that you shouldn't break magic mirrors."

Salem shrugged. "Works for me."

"But his lesson was better. And it's a lesson I'll never forget." She held up her hand. "I will never succumb to the temptation to put mortals in danger for any reason."

"Whatever," Salem said. "I'm just a cat. I don't have to learn anything. Let's go downstairs and make something to eat. The sandwiches are hungry."

"Oh, the *sandwiches* are hungry," Sabrina drawled, amused.

"I could also do with a little something," Salem allowed. "I hate for others to eat alone. I'm thoughtful that way."

Chuckling, Sabrina left the room with Salem in tow.

In the corner of Sabrina's bedroom, one of the mirror's shards flew out of the box and positioned itself in the frame. It was the mirror face's mouth.

"Good job, girlie," it said. "Keep this up, and I'll be good as new by the end of the week."

MONDAY

The Interview
By Diana G. Gallagher

Sabrina ran into the kitchen and set Aunt Zelda's laptop computer on the table. Her aunts hadn't come downstairs yet, but Salem was on the counter, hovering over his food dish.

"Free doughnuts at the bus stop?" Salem asked. "A before-school sale at the mall or what?"

"Huh?" Sitting down, Sabrina flipped open the laptop and pointed a magical modem connection.

"You're dressed and ready for school fifteen minutes ahead of your usual zap-and-dash schedule." Salem yawned, then groaned and stretched.

"I've got to check my e-mail." Sabrina opened the on-line server program and dialed in. Normally, she did sleep in until the last minute so she had to zap herself ready and run. This morning the quality of the whole day depended on whether Hugh Jeffrey, the famous and reclusive author of the best-selling book, *The Magic Within,* had agreed to give her an interview for the school paper.

"Don't you think you should feed the cat first?" Salem asked bluntly.

Sabrina pointed without looking up from the computer screen. "You're fed."

"That was too easy." Salem looked into his dish. *No wonder!* "Pretty Kitty *Lite!* Not exactly the breakfast of champions."

"Unless they're training for a sleep-athon like you." Drumming her fingers on the table, Sabrina waited impatiently for the connection to go through. "Settle or starve."

"Starve. Lite. What's the difference?" Salem sighed, stared at the bowl, then dug in.

Sabrina leaned forward as the on-line connection was completed. She had a message from Roger Chapman, Hugh Jeffrey's agent. "Yes!"

"It's much too early to be that cheerful." Aunt Hilda shuffled in and cast a limp point at the coffeemaker. The machine sputtered, dribbled a few black drops into the pot, and stopped. Frowning, she pointed again with annoyed flourish. "Energy-saver appliance my eye!"

Sabrina read the terse reply to her e-mail request and sagged.

"Mr. Jeffrey does not do interviews. Ever. Roger Chapman."

Aunt Hilda dropped into a chair and looked at Sabrina askance. "You haven't been sipping juniper joy juice sweetened with worry-wort spores, have you?"

Stricken, Sabrina just shook her head. Her seven days of serious bad luck was going to affect her everyday mortal life, too.

"Then this is just your typical teenage manic-depressive morning." Flicking her finger over her shoulder, Hilda poured a mug of coffee and floated it over.

"A bad-luck bomb." Sabrina sighed. It had never occurred to her that an author would refuse any kind of publicity-especially since Mr. Jeffrey was in Westbridge on a promotional tour and signing at the Book Shelf that afternoon.

"What bad luck?" Aunt Zelda paused in the doorway.

"I picked the only popular author in the country who doesn't do interviews for an interview Val is planning to run in *The Lantern.*"

"I'm sure you can find another author who would jump at the chance for some good press, Sabrina. Westbridge is full of writers." Zelda pointed herself a cup of herbal tea. "Some of them are even published."

"Right!" Hilda agreed. "Let's see, there's Elmer Dawson's book, *One Hundred Corn-Stalk Craft Ideas*. The hardware store sells at least twenty copies every fall." The phone rang.

"And don't forget Elizabeth Preston's *Dismal Poems for a Dreary Day,*" Zelda said.

"Yawn much?" Rolling her eyes, Sabrina jumped

up to answer the phone. Her stomach tightened when she heard Val's voice. "Oh, hi, Val. About that interview with Hugh Jeffrey—"

"You're not going to believe this, Sabrina, but *The Chronicle* wants to reprint your interview in the Sunday edition! With a byline! Of course, *The Lantern* will have the exclusive first on Friday. This is just too cool. Hugh Jeffrey has *never* done an interview before!"

Now she tells me, Sabrina thought glumly.

Aunt Zelda sat down and turned the computer toward her. She started to type in a command, then hesitated.

"I've already told the printer we're going to need twice as many copies as usual because everyone is like dying to read it!" Val paused. "You're all set to meet him at the bookstore this afternoon, right?"

"Uh . . ." Sabrina faltered. She didn't want to pass up the opportunity for a byline in a major newspaper or disappoint Val. A bummed Val was *so* no fun. "Don't worry, Val. The interview's all set."

Aunt Zelda snapped her head around as Sabrina hung up. "According to this e-mail, you're not 'all set', Sabrina."

"I'll think of something." Zapping her books into her arms, Sabrina turned toward the door.

Zelda flipped her wrist, spinning Sabrina about and freezing her niece in place with a parental power point. "What?"

"I suspect a 'whoops' might be more appropriate." Salem chuckled.

"I hope you do think of something, Sabrina," Zelda said sternly. "As long as it doesn't involve using your magic."

"Why can't I use magic? It's just an interview!" Flopping down on the counter, Salem sighed. "For me it was *just* a global conquest."

"The Witches' Council wouldn't turn me into a cat for getting an interview!" Sabrina frowned uncertainly. "Would they?"

Zelda shrugged. "It's an invasion of mortal privacy if the subject doesn't *want* to be interviewed."

"Especially in Hugh Jeffrey's case," Hilda added. "The whole point of his book is self-empowerment. He explained why he doesn't do interviews in Chapter Ten. 'Don't Go Looking for Trouble You Can Avoid.'"

"I don't remember that part," Sabrina mumbled.

"You read it?" Zelda asked Hilda, surprised.

"*The Magic Within*?" Hilda shrugged sheepishly. "I thought it was a witch romance novel. When I found out it wasn't, I used a Speed-Reading and Retention spell and zipped through it in thirty seconds flat."

"I didn't know you had to include Retention with Speed Reading spells," Sabrina said. *That's why speed reading the book didn't work!* She had procrastinated and tried to speed read the book, but couldn't retain any information. Reading it the mortal way was working, but she wasn't up to Chapter Ten yet.

"First of all, Speed Reading spells only work for adult witches." Hilda sat back slightly. "You, my dear, shouldn't miss a word of your textbooks."

"Yeah." Sabrina sighed. "So why doesn't he give interviews?"

"Because," Hilda went on, "he refuses to set himself up to be misquoted or quoted out of context. It's a self-protection issue. But he's perfectly comfortable giving lectures."

Zelda nodded. "He's speaking to the Westbridge Literary Society at Hawthorne House today."

"Interesting." Sabrina nodded. She might be able to use that information to her advantage. Another read of the book with retention added wouldn't hurt, either.

"And, Sabrina—" Zelda added a parental power stare to the parental power point. "You *know* you can't—"

The Other Realm Rule Bearer suddenly popped in wearing a red page's outfit embroidered with gold, white stockings, and white buckled shoes. Sabrina and her aunts blinked as the dark-haired, short woman placed a stool on the floor and stood on it. The long feather on her velvet cap drooped in front of her face.

"Hear ye, hear ye! The Rules of the Realm," the Rule Bearer announced in a clipped, British accent. She blew at the feather and unfurled her scroll. "Rule number seven hundred and twenty-four. No witch may use magic to achieve phenomenal success or fame in the mortal world."

"Isn't this house call highly irregular?" Hilda asked the Rule Bearer.

"Rather!" The Rule Bearer turned her cap so the feather drooped over her ear. "And I do so *hate* having to report for duty without notice at the crack of dawn."

"The sun came up almost three hours ago," Sabrina said.

"Isn't there a rule against forcing the family cat to diet?" Salem asked hopefully.

"Not if it's for your own good." Rolling her eyes, the Rule Bearer scanned down her scroll. "Rule number four hundred and seventy-seven. No witch may use magic to rectify a situation created by a lie."

"What lie?" Sabrina asked.

"Telling Val the interview with Hugh Jeffrey is set, when it isn't?" Hilda looked at Sabrina, then cast a questioning glance at the Rule Bearer.

"Sorry. Explanations are not in my job description. I just read the rules that are selected. See." The Rule Bearer turned the scroll. Rule number four hundred and seventy-seven was highlighted in iridescent yellow.

"Oh!" Hilda said brightly. "I see Drell finally installed the upgrade."

"Thank the ancient myths! The pertinent rules

are so much easier to find now." The Rule Bearer looked back at Sabrina. "You have been officially informed of the rules pertinent to your situation. Now, if you'll excuse me, I desperately need to go blow some bubbles. This is going to be a long week." With a curt bow, she vanished.

Great. "I really gotta go. Aunt Zelda?"

Zelda pointed, removing the parental freeze spell. "Try not to get into any trouble. Anything that only magic can get you out of, honey."

"Right! Later." Sabrina popped to school.

Val was waiting by her locker. She looked miserable.

"Hey, Val. What's the matter?"

"Oh, good." Val exhaled with relief. "You're still talking to me."

"We just talked on the phone fifteen minutes ago. Why wouldn't I be talking to you now?"

"Because *now* you're the hotshot reporter who's got an interview with Hugh Jeffrey and a byline in a major newspaper, and I'm just the editor of *The Lantern.*"

"Well, yeah." Sabrina nodded. "But we're still friends, aren't we?"

"If you say so!" Bubbling over with uncool joy, Val glanced at a trio of senior girls walking by. "Sabrina Spellman is my best friend," she announced.

"Way!" One of the girls gave her a thumbs-up.

"Brag much?" another girl asked.

"Brag?" Bewildered, Sabrina looked at Val askance.

"You didn't think I was going to keep the literary coup of the year a secret, did you? Get real!" Val nudged Sabrina as Libby came down the hall.

Sabrina braced herself, but the scowling Libby walked by without saying a word. "What? No cruel and caustic comment slinging at ten paces this morning?" Sabrina asked with a raised eyebrow. "I may go into insult withdrawal." Sabrina paused, then brightened. "Nope. Guess not!"

"Sabrina!" Mr. Kraft hurried down the hall. "Just the girl I wanted to see."

"Whatever it is, Mr. Kraft, I didn't do it."

"Oh, yes, you did!" Mr. Kraft smiled and patted her shoulder. "And if you need any help organizing your notes or editing the Hugh Jeffrey interview, I'll be delighted to help. I read *The Magic Within* three times. It's been a tremendous help with my work here at Westbridge High."

"Really?" Sabrina swallowed the comeback poised on the tip of her tongue. Mr. Kraft was being nice! It would be insane to point out that self-empowerment and tyranny weren't the same thing. "I'll remember that."

"Just call my pager." Mr. Kraft handed her a business card. "Of course, I'd expect to share the byline."

"That would only be fair." Sabrina nodded, smiling tightly. *"If* I need any help."

Mr. Kraft whipped his detention pad out as two boys ran by. He ran after them. "No running in the halls!"

Val looked stricken. "Tell me you're not going to collaborate with Mr. Kraft."

"Not!" Sabrina grimaced.

"Hi, Sabrina!" Grinning, Harvey sauntered over. "I hear you're serious competition for Barbara Walters all of a sudden. I mean, getting an interview with some hot author dude I've never heard of is too awesome."

"I thought *bad* news was supposed to travel fast." Sabrina frowned. It *would* be totally bad news if she didn't deliver.

Sabrina couldn't keep her mind on math during first period. Her seven days of bad luck had served up a double whammy. Hugh Jeffrey didn't give interviews and she couldn't use magic to change his mind. *But* nobody had said she couldn't use magic to get close to him. Then she might be able to *talk* him into changing his mind.

Sabrina hit the pay phones between classes and called the Hawthorne House. The desk clerk informed her that Hugh Jeffrey was scheduled to speak to the Westbridge Literary Society at one o'clock in the Seven Gables Room.

"What's he doing for lunch?" Sabrina asked.

"I'm not at liberty to divulge any information about our guests," the desk clerk said sternly.

Maybe not, but you just confirmed he's staying there! She had found out where Hugh Jeffrey was staying without using magic, just like a mortal journalist. Rising to the no-magic challenge, she tracked down Mr. Kraft between second and third periods.

"I need a pass to leave school at lunch, Mr. Kraft. Mr. Jeffrey is speaking to a local literary group and it might give me some additional insight. I don't want to screw up 'cause I ask the wrong questions, you know?"

"Excellent thinking, Sabrina!"

Sabrina nodded as Mr. Kraft scribbled on his pink-pass pad. She had never been in his office before unless she was in trouble. Delighted with her change in status, she played the vice-principal as finely as Aunt Hilda played her violin. She needed all the permission-granted time away from school she could get. "I'll have to walk to the Hawthorne House and back again."

"Oh, right. I'd drive you, but I don't dare leave during lunch. Food fights are so disgusting." Mr. Kraft arched an eyebrow. "An extra hour should do it."

"Maybe I should go home and change into something more suitable, too. What do you think, Mr. Kraft?" Sabrina stood up for inspection. As she expected, Mr. Kraft rejected the casual V-neck tee and short skirt she was wearing.

"Another hour." Mr. Kraft peered at her over the rim of his glasses. "Do you *own* anything suitable?"

"Oh, yes." Sabrina nodded vigorously as she took the pass. "Don't worry."

"Don't worry?" Mr. Kraft sighed as Sabrina left. "In my dreams."

During fourth-period study hall Sabrina finished *The Magic Within*, paying particular attention to Chapter Ten. Hugh Jeffrey valued his privacy so much he wouldn't even allow his picture to be printed on the book jacket. That way, he avoided having to deal with fans who recognized him in public places.

After fourth period, Sabrina ditched her books in her locker, ducked into the restroom, and popped to the Hawthorne House. Concealed behind a support pillar on the front veranda, she peered through a front window. The lobby in the huge, renovated mansion was small, but tastefully decorated. A cozy grouping of two wing-backed chairs and a Victorian settee around a low table dominated the center. Original seascapes and landscapes hung on the wooden panel walls. The registration desk was tucked into a small alcove and manned by a clerk wearing a visor and old-fashioned garters on the sleeves of his white shirt. Two middle-aged women stylishly dressed in tailored suits walked out of a room off the lobby and went into the ladies' room.

Sabrina glanced at her reflection in the glass. A teenaged girl in a room full of matronly women and older gentlemen was bound to raise curious eyebrows and arouse suspicion. With a flick of her finger, Sabrina changed into a blue suit with a white blouse and plain, low-heeled pumps, wrapped her hair into a secure, but stunning, French twist, topped it off with a wide-brimmed hat and aged herself twenty years. She grimaced when she saw herself in the window. Not bad for thirty-seven, but she sure hoped her finger didn't develop any weird witch diseases that could prevent her from changing back.

On her way through the lobby, Sabrina overheard the desk clerk and a distinguished-looking man talking. She stopped and pretended to rummage through her bag so she could eavesdrop, another mortal journalistic ploy.

"Please have Mr. Jeffrey's order delivered to his room precisely at two," the distinguished man said. "He has a book signing at four and hates to be rushed."

"Yes, sir." The clerk nodded. "I'm sure you'll find the room-service staff at the Hawthorne is prompt and efficient."

More ammunition if I need it. Sabrina smiled as she walked toward the Seven Gables Room. A woman seated at a card table by the door stopped her.

"Are you a new member? Do you have an invitation?"

"Uh—yes! Yes, I am." Sabrina glanced at the stack of embossed invitations the woman had already collected, then pointed into her bag and pulled out a reasonable facsimile.

"And your name is—?"

"Sa—uh, Savannah Georgia." With a demure nod, Sabrina walked into the room and took a seat in a corner. Hugh Jeffrey stepped behind the podium exactly at one o'clock.

Tall and trim with graying hair, Hugh Jeffrey had an eccentric, yet scholarly air about him. He held himself stiffly erect and looked like Sabrina's image of a writer in a tweed jacket with suede elbows, a black turtleneck, and faded jeans.

He also was boring.

He spoke for fifty minutes in a sleep-inducing monotone without once making eye contact with the audience. He also didn't say anything he hadn't already written in his book.

When he finished, Sabrina straightened up in her chair, anticipating the usual question and answer session that followed such lectures. She was ready. However, Mr. Jeffrey simply nodded to the room full of fans and left.

"I'm so disappointed," an elderly woman at the next table said to a younger woman beside her. "But then, considering Chapter Ten, I'm not surprised he wouldn't answer questions. I know Mildred was planning to ask him something dreadfully personal." She chuckled.

The other woman nodded, thoughtfully. "Maybe there's more to it than just avoiding unnecessary trouble. What if he stutters when he gets nervous or something?"

Or maybe it's a publicity gimmick! Sabrina mulled that over as she slipped back into the lobby. Hugh Jeffrey got an enormous amount of publicity because his silence provoked speculation. Giving an interview would ruin the mysterious aura that surrounded him.

Feeling more and more like a journalist on the trail of a dynamite story, Sabrina went in search of the kitchen. She paused outside the double doors in a hall off the dining room and peeked through a small window. The chef placed a silver cover over a hamburger and fries and motioned to a young man in a waitstaff uniform. Sabrina pushed the door open slightly.

"Take this to room thirty-five," the chef said. "Just put the cart in the room and leave. I've already been assured your tip will be substantial as long as you don't chit-chat with Mr. Jeffrey."

Nodding, the young man pushed the cart toward the doors.

"Is there a problem, ma'am?"

"Problem?" Sabrina looked back at the stern maitre d' looming over her shoulder. "No. No problem. I just like to know where my food comes from."

Lame much, Sabrina?

"Most of it comes from barns, oceans, and farms." The man didn't crack a smile, but Sabrina laughed nervously.

"Would you like a table?" The man asked dryly

51

and motioned Sabrina aside as the room-service waiter pushed Hugh Jeffrey's lunch cart through the double doors.

"Sorry. I don't do lunch." Sabrina wrinkled her nose. "It's so terribly bad for the digestion." With the man's suspicious stare boring into her back, Sabrina left to catch the room-service waiter.

"Hold that elevator!" Sabrina hitched up her skirt with one hand and held on to her hat with the other as she bolted across the lobby. She dashed inside the lift just as the doors closed and skidded to a halt. She noticed that the young man was trying not to laugh and realized she still looked like a refined thirty-seven, who had just run an unladylike twenty-yard dash through the quaint and exclusive inn. "If it wasn't for chasing elevators, I wouldn't get any exercise at all!"

"Floor, ma'am?"

"Three." The instant the elevator stopped on the third and top floor, Sabrina froze time. She zapped herself back into a teenager wearing a Hawthorne House waitstaff uniform, then pried the immobile young man's fingers off the handle of the cart. Taking a deep breath, she pointed.

"Man and lift in limbo stay
I'll be back sometime today!"

With the elevator frozen and inoperative, Sabrina popped the cart into the third floor hallway and headed for room thirty-five. Her watch read

1:58. She paused before the door and waited until exactly two o'clock before knocking.

"Room service." Seconds passed and no one answered. "Room service!" More seconds passed. Sabrina knocked and the unlatched door swung open. "Hello?"

Hugh Jeffrey stood in the middle of the room, staring at her.

"Oh, sorry! The, uh—, door just opened when I knocked." Sabrina winced uncertainly. "Room service?"

Mr. Jeffrey just stared. He didn't look angry. He looked terrified. His eyes widened suddenly. "Roger!"

"Over and out?" Sabrina blinked, mystified by the bizarre and awkward situation.

The distinguished man Sabrina had seen at the registration desk burst into the room. "Hugh! I'm so sorry I didn't get back before room service arrived. One of the elevators is stuck!"

Sabrina stepped aside as the distinguished looking man, who apparently was Roger Chapman, Mr. Jeffrey's agent, rushed past her to the speechless author.

Composing himself, Hugh Jeffrey nodded. "Quite all right, Roger. Not your fault."

Sabrina started as Mr. Jeffrey turned his back and sighed heavily.

He's shy!

Mr. Chapman turned to Sabrina. "Just leave Mr. Jeffrey's order and go, please."

Might as well leave. Sabrina sighed. Roger Chapman wasn't going to let anyone near Hugh Jeffrey. Besides, the real waiter would be in big trouble if anyone found out the cart destined for the author's room had been stolen.

"Jeffrey? Uh-oh. I've got the wrong room! See ya!"

Sabrina pulled the cart back into the hall, slammed the door, and popped back into the elevator. She positioned the cart in front of the young man, then changed back into her thirty-seven-year-old self and unfroze time. The waiter was totally unaware that anything strange had happened. His delay would be blamed on the stuck elevator.

"After you," the young man said when the lift doors opened.

"I'm not getting off. I forgot something."

Sabrina pondered the unsettling encounter with Hugh Jeffrey as the elevator descended. Now she knew the real reason he didn't give interviews or answer questions and spoke in a monotone without looking at his audience. He was shy in the extreme. Totally people-phobic.

But that's not my problem.

She had to get an interview.

Sabrina's resolve was cemented when she returned to school and Mrs. Quick stopped her in the hall.

"I just came from a meeting with Mr. Kraft."

The math teacher and faculty advisor for *The Lantern* practically jiggled with excitement. *"The Chronicle* is thinking of doing a companion piece about you and Westbridge High!"

"Cool!" Sabrina grinned. "So I'll get my picture in the paper, too?"

"Uh-huh. They want a shot of you and Mr. Kraft, your mentor and inspiration."

Bummer.

Sabrina spent the last period of the day considering her options, which, she finally concluded, were limited to one.

Magic.

She was sure the Witches' Council wouldn't punish her for using magic to help someone. So what if she inadvertently benefited, too. Like the Rule Bearer had told her when Drell had turned Jenny into a grasshopper, there were more loopholes than there were rules. *And I've found a loophole!*

Sabrina arrived at the Book Shelf at 3:40—twenty minutes ahead of Hugh Jeffrey and his protective agent—and got into the line that was just starting to form. When she reached the autographing table, it would be easy to cast an Antishyness spell. With that obstacle removed, she was sure the author would *want* to be interviewed.

"Ahem." The Rule Bearer had popped into line behind her with her stool and scroll. "The Rules of the Realm!"

"Are you crazy?" Sabrina panicked until she saw that everyone else in line was frozen.

"Rule number two hundred and forty-eight. All personality traits altered by magic shall be temporary."

"What's the definition of temporary?" Sabrina raised a hopeful eyebrow.

"That depends on the variables," the Rule Bearer said, rolling up her scroll. "Fifteen seconds to fifteen years. There's no way to know."

"You're a big help."

"I probably shouldn't have told you that much. I'm not supposed to explain. I just—"

Sabrina interrupted. "I know. You just—"

Time returned to normal when the Rule Bearer popped out.

"Read the rules."

"Were you talking to me?" The young man standing in line behind Sabrina looked at her with dark, brown eyes. He brushed a renegade lock of light brown hair off his forehead, then added with a boyish grin, "I hope."

"Uh—" *Why not?* Sabrina thought. They both had time to kill before Hugh Jeffrey arrived. She tapped the copy of *The Magic Within* he had tucked under his arm. "What did you think of it?"

"How long have you got?" His grin broadened.

"About fifteen minutes."

"That's enough." He extended his hand. "Josh Carter, aspiring novelist."

"A writer! Cool." Sabrina shook his hand and

introduced herself. "I'm a student. Currently thinking about a career in journalism."

"Your chances of making it are probably better than mine, then."

"Why do you say that?" Sabrina asked.

"Habit." Josh laughed when Sabrina blinked. "That's what I used to say, before I read *The Magic Within.*"

"Really. What difference did the book make?"

"For starters?" Josh sighed. "If it wasn't for Hugh Jeffrey, I might have given up the one thing I love to do most in the world."

"Writing?" Sabrina frowned, confused and curious. "Why would you even *think* about giving up something that means so much to you?"

Josh tilted his head back and laughed softly. "Well, for one thing, selling a first novel isn't easy and it takes years before the lucky few can make a living writing fiction. Add in parents and girlfriends who think trying to satisfy a dream against those odds is foolish and irresponsible and you begin to wonder if it's worth the effort."

"But how did Mr. Jeffrey's book help?" Sabrina's frown deepened as the line began moving into the store.

"In a nutshell, he said that people have to be honest *and* true to themselves—regardless of what the rest of the world thinks." Josh smiled. "I honestly don't want to do anything but write, so that's what I'll do. Even if I have to wait tables or dig ditches to support myself while I'm doing it."

"So you haven't actually sold a book or anything, yet."

"Actually, I've had two short stories published. The pay barely covered a couple of electric bills, but—" Josh shrugged. "Nobody's shown much interest in my novel, yet, though."

"Well, two published stories is awesome!" Sabrina was genuinely happy for him, but another question suddenly came to mind. "But doesn't your decision to be a writer contradict Chapter Ten? 'Don't Go Looking for Trouble You Can Avoid.' I mean, your parents probably aren't thrilled."

"Not now, no. But if I stick to my guns like Mr. Jeffrey suggests, eventually they'll realize that by doing the right thing for me, I did the right thing for everyone. I might be poor, but I'll be happy. I mean, what parent wants to talk to a son who's always miserable?"

"Good point." Sabrina started when she saw how quickly the line was moving.

"I mean, Mr. Jeffrey *never* gives interviews," Josh added. "His reasons don't matter. It's the right thing for him *not* to do. Get it?"

"Yeah. I do. Unfortunately." Only two people stood between Sabrina and the autographing table set up by a huge display of the best-selling book. Her mind reeled. If she tricked Mr. Jeffrey into granting her an interview, his credibility would be ruined.

She stepped out of line and left the store. She could hear Josh calling her name.

Numb, Sabrina sat on a bus stop bench and stared at the street. She wasn't anxious to face Val or Mr. Kraft or Mrs. Quick and definitely not Libby.

"Just my luck to have aunts who raised *me* to have principles! And a heart."

"At least, you won't be a cat when you go beddy-bye." Dressed in a dazzling blue tee and shorts, the Quizmaster popped onto the bench beside her.

"If I was a cat, I wouldn't have to listen to Libby gloat." Sabrina threw up her hands. "I can't believe I'm passing up the chance to get an exclusive interview published in a real newspaper! With my picture and a byline and everything."

"Why did you?" The Quizmaster asked pointedly.

Sabrina exhaled shortly. "Because I didn't want to destroy Hugh Jeffrey's career. I mean, he's so shy he avoids talking to any strangers. So obviously, the empowerment methods he wrote about didn't work for him. If anyone knew that, *The Magic Within* would drop off the best-seller lists faster than a boulder off a cliff."

"And the problem with that is what?" The Quizmaster shrugged. "If his method doesn't work—"

"It doesn't work for Mr. Jeffrey," Sabrina corrected. "Apparently, it works *great* for other people."

"Fair enough." The Quizmaster zapped a pair of glittering sunglasses onto his face. "But nobody *knows* he's shy."

"Not yet. But what if after he broke the 'no-interview' rule with me, he decided to try it again with someone else? Believe me, a professional reporter would notice he was a nervous, tongue-tied wreck. And all because my Anti-shyness spell had worn off." Sabrina flinched. *"If* I had used an Anti-shyness spell, which I *didn't."*

"Good thing."

"Why's that?" Sabrina scowled.

"Can't say." The Quizmaster slapped his knees and stood up. "Gotta go. What are you going to do now?"

"Turn myself into a snake, crawl under a rock, and hibernate until spring? Maybe by then no one will care about this fiasco."

"Here's a friendly bit of advice." The Quizmaster leaned over and whispered before he popped out. "Work an angle."

"What angle?" At a loss, Sabrina glanced back toward the store as Josh Carter walked out with his nose in the pages of *The Magic Within*. She jumped up and ran toward him, waving. "Hey! Josh! Wait up!"

"Hi, Sabrina! How come you ducked out so fast?"

"I left my copy of the book in my locker. And—

I've got this problem. You could help me out, though!"

"Maybe. What's the problem?"

"I'd like to interview you as an aspiring writer who's been inspired by *The Magic Within* for my school paper."

Josh didn't hesitate to answer. "Cool! When?"

"Right now?"

Sabrina relaxed as Josh led the way toward his favorite coffeehouse. He wasn't Hugh Jeffrey, but she'd have a published-author interview for Val to run in the Friday edition of *The Lantern*. And if she wrote it well enough, maybe *The Chronicle* would still consider running it. Then, if nothing else, the publicity might help Josh sell his novel.

All things considered, her bad luck could have been worse.

On the other hand, there were five more days to go.

Another shard of glass settled back into place in the corner of the mirror.

TUESDAY

Smitten
By Ray Garton

Sabrina had never liked Tuesday. It wasn't a particularly bad day of the week, like Monday, which officially killed the weekend and sent everyone back to school. But it wasn't a particularly good day of the week, either, like Friday, which marked the end of the week and ushered in the freedom and relaxation of the weekend. Even Wednesday was preferable to Tuesday because it was "hump day," the day that marked the middle of the week, after which it was all downhill to the weekend.

Tuesday was just a useless day, the day between the worst day of the week and "hump day." It was a nothing day. But this particular Tuesday was worse than usual. It held an annoyance level somewhere between Sunday night and Monday morning, but with more pain.

Sabrina limped to her locker because her right

foot hurt. The others in the hall passed her by like the water of a river rushing around a snagged log.

That morning, a large moth had gotten into the house and terrorized Salem. Either the moth had actually been chasing Salem, or Salem had mistakenly run in all the directions the moth had planned to go. Either way, the scaredy-cat had shot into the kitchen while Sabrina was pouring herself a glass of orange juice, jumped onto the counter, and knocked the toaster onto her foot.

"Ouch!" Sabrina had cried. "That hurt, Salem!"

"Help! Help!" Salem had shouted as he ran through the sink, hopped up to the counter, and then dropped to the floor again. "Moth! Moth! Get this thing off me!"

Sabrina had leaned against the counter and held her throbbing foot as she watched Salem run from the moth. "I hope he eats your coat!" she'd called with a groan of pain in her voice.

Her foot still hurt, which was why she was limping. On top of that, she'd zapped the snooze button one too many times and she'd overslept. The glass of orange juice she'd been pouring when Salem had knocked the toaster on her foot had been the only breakfast she'd gotten that morning. So, Sabrina was not only in pain, she was hungry.

She opened her locker, then looked down at her aching foot. Sabrina considered casting a spell to kill the pain, but she wondered if her injured foot was a test. *Maybe I'm* supposed *to have a sore foot, and maybe I'm supposed to put up with it?* There was no way to know. *What a goofy week!*

Sabrina sighed heavily as she took from the locker the book she needed for her first class. She was about to slam her locker door shut, just because she felt like slamming something, when she felt a hand on her shoulder and spun around, startled.

"Boy, you're jumpy," Valerie said. "Drink a lot of coffee this morning?"

"Oh, no, no, I'm just, uh . . . nothing," Sabrina said, shaking her head. She closed her locker door.

"Well, if you're having a bad day, it's about to get worse," Valerie said.

"What do you mean?"

Valerie poked a thumb over her shoulder and asked, "Who do you suppose that is?"

Sabrina's eyes followed the direction of Valerie's thumb and fell on Mr. Kraft walking down the hall. The students crowding the hall parted before Mr. Kraft like the Red Sea parting before Charlton Heston.

Walking beside the vice-principal was a girl Sabrina had never seen before. She looked the same age as Sabrina and Valerie, but was taller, with long, thick black hair, an olive complexion, and large, beautiful eyes. Everything about her was beautiful, right down to her knock-out figure in boot-cut pants and a crocheted top.

Mr. Kraft talked to the girl as they walked slowly down the hall. He was even smiling. Mr.

Kraft never smiled . . . unless he was disciplining a student.

Valerie leaned close to Sabrina and asked, "Do you think they're teaching supermodel classes here now?"

"Even if they are," Sabrina replied, "I don't think she needs to take any."

Guys stumbled over their own feet as they passed the raven-haired beauty, gawking at her in awe. The girls in the hall glared at the stranger like jungle cats eyeing an intruder that was creeping into their territory. Everyone in the hall noticed the girl, and a few guys collided with one another while watching her.

"You think she's a new student?" Valerie asked.

"Either that, or Mr. Kraft has started giving tours of the campus to students from other schools."

Valerie frowned at Sabrina. "Well, that would be silly."

"You asked a silly question. Of course she's a new student, why else would Mr. Kraft be showing her around?"

"Maybe she's, like, a relative, or something," Valerie suggested. "You know, maybe she's his niece, and he's just showing her where he works."

Sabrina shook her head. "I'm pretty sure it's impossible for Mr. Kraft to be related by blood to anyone that pretty."

"Hey, you two, what's up?"

Sabrina and Valerie turned to see Harvey smiling at them as he opened his locker.

Valerie replied, "Oh, we were just watching the—"

Sabrina poked her in the ribs with an elbow, and Valerie swallowed her words. When Valerie gave her a confused look, Sabrina shook her head slightly, then turned to Harvey and said, "Watching the time fly by until the first bell rings."

He glanced at her and chuckled as he put a couple books in his locker. "Are you in a goofy mood this morning, or what?"

More like "or what," Sabrina thought.

She wasn't sure why she'd kept Valerie from pointing out the new girl to Harvey. After all, Sabrina and Harvey weren't together anymore. Sure, they still went out once in awhile, but usually with others, never as boyfriend and girlfriend. They'd backed off from that, but that didn't mean Sabrina didn't think about it anymore. She often missed their relationship as it had been, and still had strong feelings for Harvey. But that was no reason for such jealous behavior . . . was it?

Of course it was. She knew exactly why she didn't want Harvey to notice the new girl. Because the girl was so beautiful she was turning all the other guys in the building into drop-jawed clods, and Sabrina was afraid she would do the same thing to Harvey. It was bad enough that Libby had been trying to snag Harvey for herself the last few months; Sabrina wasn't up to seeing a total stranger succeed at it with a single look.

Harvey took a book from his locker, then closed it. He walked with Sabrina and Valerie. Sabrina was relieved that they were walking away from the new girl and Mr. Kraft.

"Oops," Harvey said, stopping suddenly. "Forgot the chapter notes I made last night."

Sabrina watched him as he turned and headed back to his locker. Before he got there, Harvey came to an abrupt halt, staring directly at the girl. *Uh-oh!* He stood there for a long moment, his back to Sabrina. "Wow," he muttered. Then he said over his shoulder, "Hey, uh, look, I . . . I'll see you guys later."

Sabrina's eyes widened in amazement—and more than a little shock—as Harvey made his way through the crowded hall toward the girl. He didn't hesitate for a second, didn't stumble or wobble like the other guys in the hall. He walked with confidence and didn't stop until he was standing in front of the girl and Mr. Kraft.

"What's he doing?" Valerie whispered. Her eyes were as wide as Sabrina's.

Sabrina didn't reply. She couldn't find her voice. Instead, she just watched as the girl's lovely face lit up with a brilliant smile.

Harvey exchanged a few words with Mr. Kraft. Mr. Kraft said something to the girl and then he

walked away and left Harvey and the girl together!
They walked down the hall, both smiling as they
talked animatedly, and passed by Sabrina and
Valerie as if they weren't there. An instant before
they rounded a corner and disappeared from
sight, Harvey and the girl joined hands.

"Did . . . did I just see that?" Valerie asked.
"Or did somebody put something funny in my
Grape Nuts this morning?"

Sabrina felt her heart beating in her throat. She
couldn't believe what she'd just seen . . . and she
didn't like the sharp pang she felt in the pit of her
stomach.

"Hey, are you okay?" Valerie asked.

Sabrina realized she'd been staring at the spot
where she'd last seen Harvey and the girl. She
blinked her eyes a few times and took a deep
breath. "Sure, I'm fine," she said, smiling at
Valerie.

"Really? 'Cause you look upset. You, uh . . .
you and Harvey haven't, like, started dating
again, have you?"

"No, nothing like that."

"Well, even so, it's pretty amazing, seeing him
walk off with a total stranger like that. I wouldn't
blame you if you were . . . well, you know, a little
hurt."

Sabrina started walking, and Valerie fell into
step beside her.

"How come you're limping?" Valerie asked.

"Oh, it's nothing. I hurt my heart, is all."

Valerie stepped in front of her, forcing her to stop. "You hurt your what?"

When Sabrina realized what she'd just said, she quickly corrected it as her face grew hot with embarrassment. "Foot, I meant I hurt my foot. Salem knocked the toaster on it this morning."

Valerie cocked head and squinted at Sabrina suspiciously. "Are you sure you're all right?"

The shrill peal of the first bell of the day echoed through the halls.

"Yeah, I'm fine," Sabrina fibbed with a smile. "C'mon, let's get to class."

This is my bad luck.

Throughout the first class of the day, Sabrina could not concentrate. She was too busy eyeing the door, waiting for Harvey to come in late. But by the end of the class, the door had not opened, and Harvey's seat was still empty.

On the way out of the classroom, three people asked Sabrina why she was limping. She gave them perfunctory replies as she limped out of the room and into the hall.

"You know, for somebody whose foot got smashed by a toaster, you're moving pretty fast," Valerie said, catching up with her.

Sabrina stopped in the hall and looked in both directions for Harvey. She spotted him to the left, at the other end of the hall. He was standing beside the drinking fountain while the girl got a drink. She started limping toward them, frustrated that she couldn't move any faster. It took every ounce of willpower she had not to zap herself over there with her magic.

"Our next class is in the *opposite* direction," Valerie pointed out as she walked along with Sabrina.

"I know. I just thought it would be nice to meet Harvey's new friend." Sabrina smiled and sounded pleasant in spite of the knot in her stomach. She tried to ignore it because it was so silly. She didn't want to be one of those jealous girls who get upset when their ex-boyfriends start seeing someone else, but there wasn't much she could do about it. "Don't you think?"

"Sabrina, you're starting to worry me."

"Why?"

"Your smile—if it gets any bigger, the top of your head's gonna come off. You really are upset, aren't you?"

"Don't be silly."

Up ahead, the girl stepped back from the drinking fountain and she and Harvey began to walk away. Sabrina knew she'd never catch up with him at the rate she was going, so she called, "Hey! Harvey!"

He stopped, looked back, and smiled at her. "Hey, Sabrina," he said cheerfully. "I'll see you at lunch, okay?" He waved at her, then put his arm around the girl's shoulders as they disappeared around the corner.

"Whoa!" Valerie exclaimed. "That Harvey's becoming quite an operator!"

Sabrina wanted to say something cool and witty, but she just couldn't think of anything. She was struck with a sudden urge to cast a spell—a spell that would make Harvey instantly lose all interest in the beautiful stranger who had come out of nowhere and stolen his heart before it could beat twice. But she couldn't think of an appropriate spell. She needed her spellbook, which was in her bedroom at home.

Sabrina turned and started walking back in the direction from which they'd come. "You go ahead, Valerie. I'm gonna hit the rest room."

"Want me to come with you?"

"Nah. After seventeen years of practice, I can manage." Sabrina laughed, but it was forced.

"Okay, see you in a few."

In the rest room, there were a couple girls standing at the mirror. Sabrina went to the last stall and closed and locked the door. She stood there and listened to the girls chatter for about half a minute, until they finally left. The rest room was dead silent . . . empty. Sabrina waved her hand through the air—

And was standing in her bedroom an instant later. She got her spellbook from the shelf and flopped onto her bed to find what she was looking for.

"Is that horrible beast gone?" Salem asked.

There was a whimpering tone to his muffled voice.

Sabrina looked around the room but didn't see him. "Where are you, Salem?"

"Under the bed."

She rolled her eyes. "You can come out. I don't see the moth anywhere."

Salem crept out from beneath the bed, looked around cautiously, then hopped onto the mattress beside Sabrina.

"Thanks to you," she said, "I've been hobbling around like Quasimodo all day."

"Sorry about the toaster. I knocked over a plant in the living room, too. Not on anyone's foot, though, just the special carpet from Merlin's castle. The one Zelda loves—"

"Don't worry about it. It probably wasn't really your fault anyway, what with all this bad luck hanging over my head. What is it with you and moths, anyway? They don't bite."

"It doesn't matter. It's those creeply little things sticking out of their heads and those awful powdery wings, and . . ." Salem's whole body quaked with a disgusted shudder. "How come you're home so early?"

"Looking up a spell," she said, paging through the book.

"Uh-oh. Something's up. What?"

"Never mind. I don't have much time."

"Oh, come on," Salem said, walking around the

book and sitting on the other side of her. "Do you know how boring it is being a cat? Just hanging around the house all day, batting at the occasional dangling string, watching water drip from the faucet. The most fun I have is watching Hilda try to find the television's remote control after I've hidden it behind the beans in the pantry. C'mon . . . tell me what's happening on the outside."

As she continued to page through the book, Sabrina told Salem about the new girl at school, and about Harvey's reaction to her.

"Wow," Salem said. "Holding hands only seconds after meeting. Sounds like true love to me."

"Hey, I feel bad enough already, if you don't mind."

"So, what are you looking for in the spellbook?"

"A spell."

The cat sighed. "Okay, I asked for that one. What *kind* of spell?"

She turned her attention to the cat for a moment. "Well, I know you're gonna say it's petty, but . . ." She fell backward, lying on her bed with the spellbook open on her lap. "See, when Harvey and I decided to cool things off for awhile, I figured we'd stay close, you know, be friends, do things together, have fun. And we have. But I always thought that after awhile—sometime in our senior year, maybe, with high school almost behind us—we'd get back together. We'd just pick up where we left off, like we'd never stopped, and everything would be great. But now this girl comes along, and all of a sudden Harvey behaves as if the whole school is empty except for the two of them. He even skipped class, for crying out loud! This total stranger comes out of nowhere, and Harvey's brain melts like butter! Suddenly, I realized he and I might never get back together, that he might end up with her, and . . . and—"

"And you don't want to let that happen."

She sat up again and continued paging through the book. "Exactly."

"So you're gonna cast a spell to make him fall for you again? That's asking for trouble, Sabrina. You know the rules about using magic to make someone fall in love with you."

"That's not what I'm going to do."

"What are you going to do?"

"Aha!" Sabrina exclaimed, stabbing a page with her forefinger. "Just what I was looking for!"

"What? What?" Salem hopped up on her left shoulder and looked down at the page.

"Just something temporary, something that will bring a halt to this ridiculous love-at-first-sight fever Harvey seems to have. It's not a spell that will make him fall for me, but for someone else . . . someone other than the new girl."

"And that would be . . . ?"

"Libby."

"What? But I thought you didn't like Libby!"

"Well, I'm not one of her fans, that's for sure.

But it's Libby who's never liked me. In fact, I don't think she likes anyone. But she thinks she wants Harvey. This spell will hand him to her on a silver platter today, but it'll make him fall so hard for her that his behavior will embarrass her to tears. He'll be like a little boy with a crush on his teacher. If I know Harvey, he'll make a spectacle of himself fawning over Libby, showering her with public displays of affection, and she'll be mortified. Tomorrow it will all be over, anyway." She laughed as she read the instructions for the spell. "Yep. This'll work, all right."

"But Sabrina, if you do that, you're still breaking the rules!" Salem insisted. "You're not supposed to interfere in the lives of mortals!"

"Sometimes I'm not so sure Libby's a mortal. Most of the time she behaves like one of those harpies from mythology."

Salem dropped off her shoulder and began to pace beside her on the bed. "Maybe you should discuss this with Zelda and Hilda first—"

"Are you kidding? I don't have time for that. I have to get back to class, and I want to cast this spell before lunch." She concentrated on the book as Salem continued to pace.

"I don't know, Sabrina. This sounds like trouble to me. But then, I'm just a cat. Nobody ever listens to me. I could come up with a cure for the common cold, but it wouldn't do anyone any good because no one ever listens to cats. I could invent the perfect—"

Sabrina reached over and tugged on Salem's fur.

"Oowww!"

"Sorry," she said.

"What was that for?"

"It's for the spell."

"Haven't you ever heard of scissors?"

"I'll make it up to you. When I get home from school, I'll conjure up a big bowl of tuna. How's that?"

"I'd rather have a big bowl of tuna salad from Carnegie Deli. Best tuna salad in the world."

"You've got a deal. Now, let's see . . ." Holding the fur between the thumb and forefinger of her left hand, Sabrina read the rest of the instructions. "I'm supposed to run the fur up and down the forefinger of my right hand three times as I recite the spell, then my finger is . . . loaded."

"Loaded?" Salem asked. He got up and looked at the book. "Did you read that right?"

"Uh-huh. Loaded. It'll stay that way for only one hour. If I want it to stay loaded for *two* hours, I have to use two cat—"

"Ooohhh no you don't!" Salem snapped, backing away from her. "You'll take an hour and like it!"

"Calm down. I can do this in an hour easy. Anyway, I'm supposed to zap Harvey with my finger first, and then the person I want Harvey to fall in love with, which is, of course, Libby. Now, the spell . . ." She began to run the tuft of fur up and down her right forefinger slowly as she read the words.

> *"Like Cupid's arrow, straight and swift*
> *Aim for the heart to make love shift.*
> *He'll be smitten for a day.*
> *Tomorrow it'll go away."*

Sabrina's forefinger glowed a soft, pulsating gold for a moment, then faded and became normal again.

"Be careful where you point that thing," Salem cautioned.

Sabrina closed the book and limped across the room to put it back on the shelf. "That was simple enough," she said. "Now I've got an hour to take Harvey's mind off that *Party of Five* wannabe."

"Don't say I didn't warn you," Salem drawled.

"Everything's gonna be fine, Salem. Just because I'm being bombarded with bad luck doesn't mean I have to put up with all of it. See ya." She waved her hand and disappeared in a clowd of fluttering blue sparkles.

An instant later, Sabrina found herself sitting in the dark staring at a big movie screen. Black and white figures moved over the screen in an old movie. After a few confused seconds, Sabrina recognized the movie as *Casablanca*. But what was she doing in a movie theater instead of school?

"Hey, Sabrina," a voice whispered.

Startled, she turned to her right and saw the Quizmaster. He held a large bucket of popcorn on his lap.

Sabrina looked around to see that the theater was full. "Where are we?" she hissed. "Who are all these people?"

"Oh, I just whipped them up. I hate watchin' movies alone."

"What am I doing here?"

"I intercepted your trip. I would've come to you, but I didn't wanna miss the end of the movie. I love this movie."

"Look, Quiz, I'm in a hurry, so could I just—"

"Don't worry, I won't hold you up long. I just wanted you to know there are a few things you should consider." He spoke to her in a whisper, with his eyes on the screen.

"Like what?"

He stuffed a handful of popcorn into his mouth and munched on it. "Well, for one thing, what if that loaded finger of yours hits the wrong person?"

"Have you been eavesdropping on me?"

"Hey, just doin' my job!" He held the bucket of popcorn out to her. "Want some?"

Sabrina was still very hungry from missing breakfast, so she scooped some popcorn up in her left hand and began eating it one piece at a time. "Look, don't worry," she whispered, glancing at the movie. "I'm going to be very careful."

"Well, some of the worst accidents happen while people are being very careful."

"You're as bad as Salem."

He looked at her for a moment. "Oh, yeah? Well, he's a pretty smart cat, you know."

"What's that supposed to mean?"

"I'm just saying maybe you should listen to him a little more, don't dismiss him so easily."

Sabrina sighed. "Can I go now?"

He ignored her question. "What happens if the spell wears off, but Harvey still feels the same about Libby?"

Sabrina's hand froze on its way to her mouth with a piece of popcorn. She hadn't thought of that . . . and it was a chilling thought. *But surely that won't happen . . . can't happen.*

"But that's not how the spell is supposed to work," Sabrina said. "If that happened, I think I'd have a juicy lawsuit on my hands. The whole point of doing this is to take Harvey's mind off the new girl."

"When the spell wears off, how do you know he won't go back to being crazy about the new girl?"

"Well, I . . . I . . ." Sabrina didn't like that question, because she didn't know he wouldn't still be crazy about the new girl. She was pretty sure it would work, but not positive. "Look, I know Harvey. His attention is easily diverted. That's all this is . . . a diversion. Once the spell wears off, he'll be back to his old self." By then the new girl would've moved on to another guy.

"Just keep in mind that the spell doesn't make any promises."

"Are you trying to confuse me?"

"No, not at all. Just giving you a little food for thought."

"Well, my brain isn't hungry. Can I please go now?"

"Sh-sh-sh!" he hushed, holding up a hand to her as he stared intently at the screen. "I love this ending."

On the screen, Humphrey Bogart and Ingrid Bergman stood on a misty airstrip, looking into each other's eyes. A plane waited in the background, propellers spinning.

"You better hurry, or you'll miss that plane," Bogart said.

Bergman fell into his arms and said, "No, Rick! I'm not going. I can't! You're the only man for me. I can change my mind . . . but I can't change my heart."

"Hey, wait a second, that's not right!" Sabrina whispered. "I thought Ilsa got on the plane with the other guy and left Rick behind in the end."

"Not in my theater, baby," the Quizmaster said. "I'm a happy ending kinda guy. Limp along now, Sabrina. I'll catch you later. And remember to be very careful with that finger. Some spells ricochet, you know." He waved his hand—

And Sabrina found herself back in the rest-room stall at school.

What was that *all about?* she wondered. She was

especially puzzled by the Quizmaster's remark about Salem. Had Salem been right about the spell breaking the rule of interfering with the lives of mortals? Sabrina had dismissed it with a joke, but could the cat have been right?

No, she was certain Salem was wrong. If the effects of the spell were permanent, then it would be breaking the rules. And surely that wouldn't even be *in* the spellbook. But the spell Sabrina had found in her book was only temporary and would wear off, so it wasn't really *interfering* in the lives of mortals . . . it was just messing with them a little.

She had only one hour—less than one hour by now. Sabrina left the stall and limped out of the rest room, eager to cast her spell.

She missed math class and was late for American history, but Mrs. Hecht, her history teacher, said nothing, probably because of Sabrina's obvious limp. Once she was seated, she looked around for Harvey, but he wasn't there.

Sabrina couldn't believe it. Harvey had disappeared with that girl and missed another class, and no one seemed to notice!

"Where've you been?" Valerie whispered.

"Uh, I got . . . held up."

Valerie's eyes bulged. "You were mugged? In the bathroom?"

"No, no, I mean I was . . . you know, distracted, detained . . . held up."

"Oh. Out looking for Harvey, huh?"

"I was not!"

"Well, it doesn't matter, anyway," Valerie whispered. "Mrs. Hecht said Harvey's been excused from all his morning classes by Mr. Kraft."

Sabrina's mouth dropped open.

"Would you like to share your conversation with the rest of us, Sabrina and Valerie?" Mrs. Hecht asked.

The girls sat up straight in their seats and stopped whispering, but Sabrina's jaw remained slack. Mr. Kraft had given Harvey a pass so he could go off with a beautiful girl and . . . do what? Make out in the bleachers?

She looked at the clock. There were about forty-five minutes left to the spell, and class would continue for another twenty. Earlier, Harvey had said he would see her at lunch. Sabrina hoped so, because it would be the perfect time to point her finger!

When the bell rang, Sabrina hurried out of the classroom with Valerie right beside her, talking a mile a minute as they headed for the cafeteria. Sabrina only vaguely heard her friend, because she was too busy keeping an eye out for Harvey and his new friend.

She behaves more like a girlfriend, she thought. *No, more like an instant girlfriend . . . just add eye contact and mix—*

"There they are!" Valerie pointed.

Harvey and the girl were walking down the hall

past the gym, hand in hand. Sabrina's foot was feeling a little better and she was able to walk faster than she had earlier in the day.

"What're you gonna do?" Valerie asked.

Sabrina didn't reply as she closed the distance between herself and Harvey. People kept darting back and forth between them in the hall, but a moment came when she had a clear shot at him. Sabrina lifted her right arm, pointed her finger, and popped the first half of the spell at him.

Harvey jolted, as if someone had poked him, then reached behind him to scratch a spot on his back.

Got him, Sabrina thought. *Right between the shoulder blades.*

"What was that?" Valerie asked, frowning.

"What was what?"

"You pointed."

"Oh, that. Yeah. That was me pointing. Haven't you ever seen someone point before?"

Valerie shook her head. "You're acting very strange today."

"Well," Sabrina said with a shrug, "it's a strange day."

They followed Harvey and the girl to the cafeteria. The lunch line was long but it was moving quickly, and the tables were filling up with students carrying trays of food.

"You go ahead and get in line, Valerie," Sabrina said. "I'll be with you in a minute."

"What, are you gonna stand around pointing some more?" Valerie asked.

"I don't know . . . maybe."

Valerie walked away, shaking her head again.

Harvey and his friend were going through the lunch line, leaning close together as they talked, both of them grinning like they'd just gotten a big fat whiff of happy gas. While they were getting their lunch, Sabrina scanned the noisy cafeteria for Libby.

The cheerleader was with Cee Cee and Jill, as usual. Each of them carried a tray as they looked for a table. Libby had a binder tucked beneath her right arm. *Her plans for world domination, no doubt,* Sabrina thought. *Or class president.*

Sabrina made her way around the tables, moving toward Libby and her friends, but not getting too close. She raised her arm, pointed her finger, and aimed carefully as Libby set her tray on a table. Sabrina sent the second half of the spell heading directly for Libby . . .

But the binder slipped from beneath Libby's arms and dropped to the floor. Libby bent down to pick it up, nearly disappearing behind the table. Her tray jerked to the side, as if it had been bumped.

Oops, Sabrina thought. *I hit her lunch!* As far she could tell, the spell had landed right in the middle of Libby's mashed potatoes.

Sabrina lowered her arm and looked around. No one was staring at her as if she'd lost her mind, so maybe she hadn't been seen pointing for no apparent reason whatsoever. She looked at the lunch line again. Valerie was getting her food, but Sabrina didn't see Harvey and the girl. Her eyes darted around the cafeteria, but they were nowhere to be seen. When she saw the clock, she realized time was running out. She had to cast the second half of the spell.

Libby was seated and about to start eating her lunch. Sabrina lifted her arm again, pointed her finger, and held her wrist steady with her left hand. She narrowed her eyes and prepared to cast the spell.

The Quizmaster suddenly made an unwelcome appearance in her thoughts. He'd said that some spells ricocheted. What in the world did that mean? She thought of Salem's admonishment—that she would be interfering in the lives of mortals, thus breaking one of the important laws of witchcraft.

She paused, her finger aimed directly at Libby. Her right hand trembled for just a moment. Then she shoved the annoying thoughts from her mind, took a deep, steadying breath, and was about to send a bolt of magic flying from her finger . . . when Libby disappeared.

"Sabrina Spellman?"

The new girl had stepped directly in front of her—the beautiful, raven-haired object of Harvey's affection.

Sabrina's arms dropped limply to her sides. "Uh . . . uh . . ."

The girl smiled. "I'm Bethany Martin. Harvey's told me all about you!"

"Uh . . . uh . . ."

"Bethany and I grew up together," Harvey said. Startled, Sabrina turned to her right and saw Harvey standing beside her. She'd been so involved in the spell she was about to cast that she hadn't noticed them approaching her with their lunch trays.

"Grew up together?" Sabrina asked hoarsely.

"We've known each other since kindergarten," Harvey continued. "We were best friends all the way up to sixth grade."

"Then my dad's company transferred him to Chicago," Bethany said. "I hated it the whole time we were there. My whole family did. But my dad's company was so happy with his work there that when he asked to be transferred back here, they not only said yes, they made him district manager. So, I'm back."

"I didn't even know she was coming," Harvey said. "I nearly fainted when I saw her in the hall this morning. Since we've known each other so long, Mr. Kraft excused me from my morning classes so I could show Bethany around and get her settled in."

Sabrina's head moved slowly as she looked back and forth from Harvey to Bethany and back to

Harvey again. "So, you mean, you two aren't . . . I mean, you actually know each other?"

"Since we were knee-high to a high knee," Harvey said. His smile melted away as he looked closely at Sabrina. "Hey, are you all right, Sab? You look . . . funny."

Sabrina wasn't quite all right. Her mind was racing over what she'd been assuming all morning, and over what she'd been about to do. An unexpected laugh blurted out of her mouth so suddenly, Sabrina slapped a hand over her lips to conceal it. But she couldn't. She was giddy with relief.

All this time and they were just sandbox playmates! I must be more stressed about my bad luck than I thought!

"What's so funny?" Harvey asked, smirking.

"It's very nice to meet you, Bethany," Sabrina said as she began to laugh even harder.

"Uh, Sabrina," Harvey said, "are you okay?"

She nodded, trying to compose herself. "Yeah . . . yeah, Harvey, I'm fine. Really." She finally stopped laughing and wiped a tear from her eye.

Harvey's face darkened with a frown. He swayed back and forth slightly. "Well . . . I'm not," he muttered.

Sabrina said, "What?"

Harvey began to look around the cafeteria frantically, his head jerking this way and that, eyes scanning the tables. He began to breathe heavily.

"Harvey?" Bethany said with concern. "What's wrong?"

Suddenly, Harvey dropped his lunch tray. It clattered on the floor as he hurried away from them and began weaving around the tables.

He was heading directly for Libby.

"Oh, no," Sabrina breathed.

"What?" Bethany asked.

Sabrina did not respond. Instead, she hurried after Harvey, and Bethany rushed after her.

Harvey stopped behind Libby, grabbed the back of her chair, and pulled it away from the table.

"Hey!" Libby exclaimed. "What are you doing?"

Sabrina couldn't understand what had gone wrong. Had she actually hit Libby with the second half of the spell? Had it only looked like she'd missed?

Harvey got down on his knees beside Libby.

Oh, no! Sabrina thought as she closed in on Harvey. *He's actually going to propose to her! Why didn't I think about how stupid he'd look—*

But he didn't propose. Instead, he grabbed Libby's fork and lifted a big scoop of her mashed potatoes to his mouth. As he chewed behind bulging cheeks, he moaned, "Mmmm . . . mmmm!" He took another bite and moaned some more.

"Oh, God, I love these potatoes! These are the most wonderful mashed potatoes! They're incredible!"

Sabrina had not hit Libby with the spell—she'd hit the mashed potatoes, just as she'd thought. She heaved a long sigh of relief, thankful that the spell would wear off after awhile.

"So, they were just old friends, huh?" Salem asked later that afternoon. He was on the floor in Sabrina's bedroom, dining on a bowl of tuna salad from Carnegie Deli.

"Yep. I don't think I've been so glad of anything before." She was reclining on her bed, thumbing through the latest issue of *Teen People*.

"You know," Salem said, "in the old days, there were very stiff penalties for using magic to make a guy fall in love with a side dish."

"Thank goodness the old days have come and gone," Sabrina replied.

"How's your foot?"

"Much better. How's your tuna salad?"

"The best. And kosher, too."

The Quizmaster popped into the room suddenly, standing beside Sabrina's bed. He was dressed just like Humphrey Bogart at the end of *Casablanca*: a trenchcoat and hat, with the brim pulled down in front, and a cigarette dangling from the corner of his mouth. But there was no color to him . . . he was a scratchy, flickering gray, just like the actor in the old black and white movie.

"Well," Sabrina said with a smug smile, "I got through today pretty well, didn't I?"

"Ilsa," he said, "I'm no good at being ominous, but it doesn't take much to see that the problems of one little day don't amount to a hill o' beans in this crazy week. Someday you'll understand that."

"Yeah, I know," Sabrina said. "I've still got four days to go."

"Well, here's looking at you, kid." The Quizmaster touched the brim of his hat, then disappeared.

"Ilsa?" Salem asked. "Who's Ilsa?"

Now the mirror's face had an eye. One eye. "I look like I'm winking!" she complained. "Oh, well, at least now I can see what's coming." She peered into the near future.

"Uh-oh!"

WEDNESDAY

Love Canal
By Mel Odom

Sabrina woke reluctantly from a restless sleep—and promptly dropped three feet. Luckily, the bed was beneath her and she didn't smack against the floor. Some days she thought sleepwalking would have been a much better choice of magic side-effects than floating.

Rolling over on her back, she stared up through the darkness but still couldn't see the ceiling above her. It was that dark. She felt even more tired than when she'd gone to bed.

"Can't sleep?" Salem asked from somewhere near the foot of the bed.

"No," Sabrina groaned. She knew she really needed to. Today was going to be another long day filled with the bad luck that was currently plaguing her. It was enough to make her shudder in dread. She felt miserable.

"It'll be over soon," Salem said. "At least you

don't have to do a hundred years as a cat. Now *that's* a long time."

She was finally able to see his eyes glowing in the darkness of her room, looking like twin moons. "Every day feels like a hundred years."

Salem made cat sounds of sympathy. Or maybe it was only his stomach rumbling.

"Waiting for the bad luck to happen is the worst part," Sabrina admitted. "If I could just schedule it in, get it over with, and move on with my day, maybe that wouldn't be so bad."

"It would be." Salem winked at her. "But then it wouldn't be bad luck. It would just be scheduled chaos."

"But it would only be one bad thing a day. You'd be surprised how many times I thought, *This is it, this is the bad luck.* Only to realize later I didn't know how good I had it." She shook her head at the memory of the last few days.

"I know what you need," Salem said in a suddenly enthusiastic voice.

"What?"

"A snack," Salem declared. His weight shifted on the bed in his eagerness. "Maybe you can whip up a tuna souffle or a tuna quiche. Or maybe even just tuna breakfast cakes. You wouldn't believe how much better a big stack of tuna cakes dripping in honey will make you feel."

"I'd rather not find out," Sabrina said, resisting the urge to gag. "The last thing I need is to start bingeing on food. I'll wake up one morning weighing nine hundred pounds."

"Chicken."

"Name-calling's not exactly a way to endear yourself to me," Sabrina pointed out.

"I wasn't calling *you* chicken," Salem replied. "I was just suggesting it as an alternative to tuna."

Sabrina didn't completely believe him. Salem wasn't exactly known for his empathizing nature. "No."

"Maybe something sweet?" His voice took on a more hopeful note.

"No." Rolling over, Sabrina glanced at the clock, seeing that it was 12:03 A.M. The new day, filled with some new threat of bad luck, had officially started. It was also the witching hour, and that made her feel a little better. Maybe that hour was one she'd be given bad-luck free, and she'd been sleeping through it. "Since I'm not getting any sleep, maybe a little television would help."

"Oh, *fine*," Salem complained, "throw out the cat's suggestion of a midnight snack, something you can quietly sneak out and grab without fear of retribution. Then *really* break the rules."

"Watching TV won't get me grounded," Sabrina said. "Watching *bad* TV is another thing altogether." Sabrina threw the blankets off and pulled her robe on. "Coming?"

Salem stood and stretched, lolling out his pink

tongue. "I suppose. Now that you've woken me, I can't sleep either."

Sabrina zapped them to the living room rather than taking the stairs. She never could remember which step was the squeaky one, and she was beginning to suspect her Aunt Zelda had purposefully zapped it to change places.

Planted in front of the television, she picked up the remote control and began flipping through the channels. Nothing really caught her eye. Sitcoms struck her as too cute, dramas overblown, movies too time-consuming, and even some of her favorite cartoons struck her as, well, juvenile.

Then she heard Robin Leach's voice-over on *Lifestyles of the Rich and Famous*. The program was familiar to her because her Aunt Hilda sometimes watched it, remarking some of the really cool spots the host missed, and lamenting the passage of buildings and businesses. Hilda had helped construct some of them.

"Robin Leach is covering a flood zone?" Salem asked from the doorway where he cowered.

"That's not a flood zone," Sabrina snorted. "That's Venice."

"Oh!" Salem slunk toward the couch. "Venice, Italy, nicknamed the Queen of the Adriatic." He rested his gaze on Sabrina. "That's an ocean."

"I've heard of Venice and I've heard of the Adriatic." Sabrina was interested in all things Italian—food, guys, shoes. "Venice was the home of the Moronic poets." *That* she was certain of.

The Moronic poets had definitely been covered in the curriculum.

"The Moronic poets." Salem's tone sounded doubtful. "And, pray tell, who were they?"

"Lord Somebody," Sabrina said. "He and his friends created—" She thought fast. "The limerick. Yeah, the limerick."

"The *Byronic* poets," Salem said. "Lord Byron, John Keats, and Percy Shelley."

"I heard of them."

"Percy's wife, Mary, wrote the novel *Frankenstein* at age eighteen."

"And that one I know too," Sabrina said irritably. "Big green guy. Bolts in his neck. Flat-top haircut." She grinned in triumph.

"Wrong," Salem replied. "That was Frankenstein's monster. The doctor was Frankenstein."

"Why do I get the feeling I'm suddenly on *Jeopardy!?*"

"Feed me. I can't talk with my mouth full. Find a good movie to get you over your blues and zap me up a big bowl of popcorn with catnip seasoning."

Sabrina did better than that. She zapped up a horse feedbag over Salem's head, scaled down to cat-size, and filled it with popcorn. She thought she heard a mumbled thank-you from Salem, but couldn't be sure over the sound of all the crunching.

She started to switch channels, but her attention was captivated by the panorama of beautiful alabaster buildings and the colorful gondolas traveling up and down the canals. Sidewalk cafes occupied niches thrust out over the water, and people dined under striped umbrellas near arched bridges that reached across the canals. She muted the sound, cutting Robin Leach off in mid-sentence, as an idea formed.

"What's the time difference between Massachusetts and Venice?" she asked Salem.

He shook his head reluctantly, working his face out of the feedbag. "Six hours."

"You're sure?"

He gave her that cocked head, moon-eyed glare of reproach combo that could be so devastating. "You question me? When you're planning to take over the world, do you have any idea how much knowledge you have to stuff into your head about geography, time zones, languages, probability factors, economic trade zones, and various other details?"

"No," Sabrina admitted. Trying to take over the world had gotten Salem turned into a cat for one hundred years.

"Of course you don't," Salem said. "That's why world dominion will never be a young person's game."

"Alexander the Great conquered the known world by age thirty-three." That was one fact Sabrina did remember. Although thirty-three seemed ancient to her, she knew Salem had been centuries older than that when he'd tried.

"Beginner's luck," Salem retorted. "And there's a lot more world these days." He returned his attention to the feedbag.

"So if it's," Sabrina glanced at her watch, "twelve-seventeen here, it's six-seventeen in Venice."

"Now we're on to math problems?"

"Think of it as Final Jeopardy!"

Salem crunched for a moment longer. "What have you got in mind?"

"How'd you like to go to Venice?"

"Right now?"

"They're getting started with their day over there," Sabrina stated. "I can't sleep. You're up. And if I'm going to go see the sights, I'd like a guide."

"Me?"

"Yes."

Salem shook his head and the feed bag waggled at the end of his nose. "Your aunts would ground your vacuum cleaner and make me an outdoor kitty if they found out."

"Maybe not. With all the bad luck I've been having, they might give me the sympathy vote and a slap on the wrist."

"They'll blame me."

"I'll tell them that it was my idea."

"You don't normally get ideas like this by yourself. They'd still suspect me."

"These aren't normal times," Sabrina pointed out. "I'm under a lot of stress." And she was.

School, witch license, the Slicery, Harvey, friends, the student newspaper. She still didn't know how she was going to handle that question. On top of that, there was all this bad luck. "I need to do something or I'm going to explode."

"If I stay here," Salem said, "Zelda and Hilda won't be as likely to blame me."

"They'll still suspect you." Sabrina pushed herself up from the couch, her decision made. "If you stay here, you'll miss breakfast."

Salem's eyes got even more round. "Breakfast?"

"They do serve breakfast in Venice, don't they?"

"Yes."

"We might even be able to squeeze in lunch before we get back. If we can get a table by eleven over there, it'll only be five A.M. over here. I can still be back in time to go to school."

"*And* lunch?" Salem got to his feet. "Lose the feedbag and put on my dancing shoes."

Feeling excited, Sabrina switched off the television and zapped them both back to her bedroom. She stood in front of the mirror. "What should I wear?"

"It's on the Mediterranean Sea. It might be cool at worst, but it maintains a steady and comfortable temperature year round."

"You've been watching the Weather Channel too much." Sabrina zapped up a pair of pearl-gray Capri pants, a tangerine tube top, and a charcoal-colored long-sleeve short-waisted light jacket that she left unbuttoned. She zapped her hair back in a French braid, then pointed up a pair of ultra-mod wraparound sunglasses with tangerine lenses that matched the tube top. "How's this?" She pirou-etted on her tangerine-colored platform sandals for Salem.

"Lovely. Just what I'd wear to breakfast if I still only had two feet. Let's go."

Sabrina walked to the bedroom closet and pulled out her vacuum cleaner.

"Taking the linen closet is going to be faster than flying," Salem said.

"We're not leaving yet." Sabrina pulled the vacuum cleaner over to the window and opened it.

Salem sat on his haunches on the bed, tail tucked protectively around himself. "Then where are you going?"

"To Harvey's."

The cat ducked his head and made whimpering noises. "I thought this was just going to be you and me."

"And breakfast and lunch," Sabrina said. "Yes, I know. But Harvey and I have got some problems we need to work out, and maybe this can help."

"By telling him you're a witch over breakfast in Venice?"

"No." Sabrina stood on the vacuum cleaner. "I'm not going to tell him I'm a witch."

"Then how are you going to explain the flying vacuum cleaner and going to Venice through the linen closet?"

"I'm going to tell him this is all a dream. His dream." At least, that sounded doable. And if it wasn't, she could erase Harvey's memory, hoping she didn't feel too badly about that. She made room for Salem on the vacuum cleaner, then flew it through the window.

In minutes she was at Harvey's house, knocking lightly on the second-story bedroom window. The neatly kept lawn was filled with dark shadows below her.

"Why don't you just zap us inside?" Salem asked, gazing back at the ground. "I feel like a clay pigeon floating around up here. All it takes is one trigger-happy neighbor—"

"I'm not going to invade his room," Sabrina said.

"Just interrupt his sleep. Right."

Harvey came to the window wearing faded green Westbridge High sweatpants and an old NO FEAR T-shirt. His eyes widened when he focused on Sabrina. Hurriedly, he raised the window. "Sab?"

Sabrina's heart felt that old tingle when he used his pet name for her. *Why can't I figure out what to do? Why can't love just be easy?* "Hi, Harvey. Hope I didn't catch you at a bad time."

"No. But I do have to wonder what you're doing outside my window on—on a flying vacuum cleaner?" Harvey shook his head, then smiled suddenly. "Oh man, this is really weird. I mean, this isn't really happening, is it?"

"Nope," Sabrina agreed. "You're having a dream."

"I thought that must be it." He reached up and pinched his cheek, squinting when it hurt. He looked puzzled. "I've never had a dream like this. Not even after *Revenge of the Brain-Stealers, Part 5* and an anchovy pizza."

"Talk quietly," Sabrina instructed, worrying that Harvey's enthusiastic voice might wake his parents.

"Quietly? But this is a dream, right?"

Hmmm . . . "Yes, but in your dream you don't want to wake your parents, do you?"

Harvey only had to think about that for a moment. "No way. Not if this is going to start off this interesting."

"It's going to get even better," Sabrina promised. "Have you ever thought about going to Venice?"

"California?"

"No. Italy. They have canals there instead of streets, boats instead of cars. I thought it might be fun."

"Don't you mean *I* thought it might be fun?" Harvey asked. "After all, this is my dream."

"Yes," Sabrina said, getting caught up in all the complications, and finding she was reluctant about giving Harvey all the credit. *"You* thought it would be fun."

"Cool." Then a troubled look filled Harvey's handsome face. "But I don't remember ever wanting to go to Venice, Italy. I don't think I even remember ever hearing about it."

"Dreams come from your subconscious," Sabrina said. "Subconsciously, you must have wanted to go to Venice. It'll be fun."

Harvey narrowed his eyes. "This doesn't seem like a dream in some ways. This is really weird."

"You think a secret desire to go to Venice is more weird than Sabrina floating on a flying vacuum cleaner outside your window?" Salem asked in irritation.

Sabrina wanted to point out to Salem that he wasn't exactly being helpful, but she didn't have time.

"Your cat talks, too?" Harvey asked, a grin splitting his face. "This dream really rocks."

"Yeah, and we're wasting time," Salem said. "If you don't hurry we're not going to make it back to the linen closet."

"There's no time frames on dreams," Harvey said. "They always kind of last from the time you go to sleep till you wake up."

"This one's different," Sabrina explained. "Is it okay if I pick out your clothes?"

Harvey shrugged. "Sure, I guess so. I mean, you wouldn't ask if I didn't want you to, right?"

"Right." Sabrina zapped Harvey into a pair of

khakis and a maroon and ebony pullover she'd gotten for him last Christmas.

"All right!" Harvey looked down at his clothes. "Hey, instead of sneakers, couldn't I get a pair of Doc Martens?"

"Sure." Sabrina sighed and zapped him into a pair of ankle-high walking boots.

"You sure this color's okay?"

"I'm positive," Sabrina said. She couldn't believe Harvey was being so difficult. Usually he was just a happy-go-lucky guy. "Uh, Harvey, why don't you join us on the vacuum cleaner."

"Are you sure it'll hold us all?"

"Yes."

"Okay then." Harvey clambered through the window and out onto the vacuum cleaner, which sank just a little under the additional weight before compensating.

Holding the handle, Sabrina gained altitude and headed for the Spellman house. She felt Salem warm and heavy on top of her feet. Harvey peered at the city passing below with real interest.

"Do you think if I jumped off I could fly?" Harvey asked.

"What?" Sabrina exploded.

Harvey looked at her and smiled. "In my dreams I can fly sometimes. Without a vacuum cleaner. I was wondering if this was going to be one of those times."

"No," Sabrina said, "it's not. Just hold onto the vacuum cleaner."

"Okay."

Maybe this isn't such a good idea after all, she thought as she made her final approach on her bedroom window. *Maybe I should just take Harvey home and forget the whole thing.* But she couldn't. The bad luck was really getting to her; she needed just a brief break from it.

She made a perfect landing inside her room, then put the vacuum cleaner away and guided Harvey to the linen closet. She took the fact that her aunts weren't up waiting for her as a good sign.

Harvey protested being dragged into the linen closet, but his protests were ignored by Sabrina and Salem. Thunder pealed and lightning flashed inside the room as Salem set the destination.

When Sabrina opened her eyes again, they were on a sidewalk in Venice in the early morning. The broad expanse of a canal filled with emerald green water stretched out before her, lapping at the foundation of an elegant building on the other side. Clothing suspended from lines strung between that building and the one next to it flapped in the gentle breeze. The acrid smell of fish nipped at her nose.

"Cool!" Harvey exclaimed. "We're here." He walked to the canal's edge and peered down. "Can we get in some fishing while we're here?"

"I thought we might go shopping," Sabrina said.

"Wait," Salem argued, "there was something mentioned about breakfast."

"Later," Sabrina told him.

"Shopping?" Harvey said, turning around. "But this is my dream. Shouldn't I be doing what I want to do?"

Sabrina thought fast. People passed around them curiously, but not pausing to look too long. Obviously the locals were used to tourists being up and about early in the day. "Sure, it's your dream," she told Harvey. "But you took the time to dream me into it. Doesn't that mean you'd want to do some things I'd want to do?"

Harvey grimaced.

"Oh, you're good," Salem whispered appreciatively.

Actually, Sabrina felt pretty crummy about it. *Even if I am experiencing the worst luck of my life and don't know how to handle my love life, there's no reason to take it out on Harvey.* Harvey interrupted her apology.

"Hey, you're right," he said. "Where would you like to go?"

His sudden change of heart didn't sit well with Sabrina either. The whole "dream" date was starting to make her feel guilty. Although she hadn't been able to sleep, she knew she'd woken Harvey from his, and he'd definitely be feeling tired the next day. He wasn't even going to know he'd really been there with her.

"Maybe fishing wouldn't be so bad," she said.

"What?" Salem leaped lithely to the top of the railing, then balanced precariously as a low-riding boat filled with people sped by and churned white waves in the water. "Are you forgetting about breakfast?"

"No, Sab." Harvey took her hand in his. "Why would I want to waste my first terrific dream of going to Venice with you by fishing? Let's go look around. Then I just hope I can remember it in the morning."

"Trust me," Sabrina said. "This is one dream I think you'll remember in the morning." She squeezed his hand, then took a look at the build-ings around them.

The structures all had similar coloring, kind of a yellowed ivory color that looked like it had been beaten into the stone by the sun and the salt spray from the sea. Of varying heights, they ranged from three to five stories tall. Nearly all of them had tall, arched windows edged in white, and small balconies where a few people stood and talked or drank coffee.

"Wow," Harvey said, pointing. "Look at that big dome."

Actually, there were two big domes set close together. They were bleached off-white by the elements as well, and topped by towers with smaller domes crowned with crosses.

"What is that place?" Sabrina asked.

"Search me," Harvey stated.

"It's a church," Salem answered. "The Santa Maria della Salute. We're standing on a sidewalk overlooking the Grand Canal. You could say it's the main drag of Venice. A little further on is the Palace of the Doges. They're the rulers of Venice."

"Cool," Harvey said. "You know, your cat's pretty smart in my dream. I thought all he did was lay on the couch and whine for food."

"Since fishing is out," Salem said, bracing himself to pounce, "have you thought about a nice *swim?*"

Moving quickly, Sabrina stepped between Salem and Harvey. "Breakfast," she reminded the cat.

"When?" he asked, not breaking from the pose.

"Do you know a place by the palace?"

"Giorgio's," Salem replied without hesitation.

"Then that's where we'll go."

Salem leaped from the railing to the sidewalk and took the lead. "It's a long walk."

"Why don't we take one of those boats?" Harvey asked, pointing at a gondola tied up near one of the many red-and-white-striped barber poles standing in the water at the canal's edge.

"How expensive are they?" Sabrina asked.

"It's a cab," Salem said. "Therefore, it's a luxury. Luxuries are always somewhat expensive. And they get in the way of breakfast *spending,*" he added.

"I'll pay for it," Harvey offered, reaching into his back pocket for his wallet. "Hey, there's only the five bucks in there that I had yesterday. I figured since this was a dream there'd be more." He folded the wallet and started to put it away.

"Why don't you check again?" Sabrina suggested. She pointed at his wallet, zapping the money from home that she'd put away to start working on her summer wardrobe. Although she could zap up new clothes to wear, she wasn't able to zap name-brand clothing. That had to be purchased, and she'd been saving some from her odd jobs.

"Wow," Harvey said, "now there's sixty-five bucks here!"

The extra sixty was all Sabrina had. *There's definitely going to be lean times ahead.*

"Do they take American money here?" Harvey asked, flipping through the money again.

"It's a dream, remember? If you need Italian money, it'll be Italian money." Sabrina zapped again, hoping the spell could cover her own lack of knowledge.

Harvey read the money, seeing the swell of colors. "Lire? Okay, cool. Let's go grab a boat." He took Sabrina by the hand and dashed down the stone steps to the waiting gondola. Sabrina barely managed to keep up with him.

"The *vaporetti* will be cheaper," Salem suggested as he bounded after them.

"What's that?" Sabrina asked.

"The motorboats with all the people in them. They call them *vaporettis,* which is kind of a water taxi."

The gondola driver eyed them hopefully. "Signore," he said. "Signorina." He kept talking, but Sabrina didn't understand him. Quickly, she zapped a spell on Harvey and herself that would allow them to speak the language.

> *"Language of Italy*
> *Language we really need*
> *Fly to our lips*
> *And help us to read"*

"Could I interest you in a ride?" the gondola owner asked.

"No thanks," Sabrina said. "We'll take the water taxi."

He smiled and nodded, then began calling out to other passersby.

"Cool," Harvey said. "I can understand him now. Am I speaking Italian?"

Sabrina couldn't tell, actually, because of the nature of the spell. However, Harvey's words did have a lyrical quality that hadn't been there before. "Yes," she replied.

They loaded into the *vaporetti,* taking seats near the back. When the craft got moving again, water splashed up on the Plexiglas windows. Sabrina took the camera she'd just zapped into her backpack and started taking pictures. The broken mirror crossed her mind only occasionally.

The *vaporetti* ran its route, and there was enough to see that Sabrina had to change film rolls in the camera twice. They got out at a landing in front of the Palace of the Doges, momentarily caught up in a wave of fellow tourists.

The palace looked like a fairy-tale creation. It was constructed of pink and white marble that gleamed in the early morning sunlight. Sabrina suspected that the morning dew and the mist off the Grand Canal had a lot to do with the effect.

"Where are we?" she asked Salem, who was now riding in her backpack.

"This is called Piazza San Marco," the cat answered. "Or, in English, St. Mark's Square. It's the civic center of Venice." He gestured with a paw to the building next to the palace. "That's the Campanile."

Sabrina took more pictures.

"Let's go," Salem said impatiently. "Giorgio's is this way." He lept from the bag and padded through the sparse morning crowd.

"He's in a big hurry," Harvey commented.

"He always is when there's food involved," Sabrina replied, starting after Salem.

"I can't believe I'm letting a cat guide me," he told her. "I must be having flashbacks to *Alice in Wonderland*. The Cheshire cat was always my favorite character."

Even though Salem's behavior left something to

be desired, Sabrina was feeling good about the whole "dream" date. The bad luck might be out there lurking somewhere, but it was back in Westbridge—not in Venice. She reached out for Harvey's hand as he caught up with her. Then immediately wondered if it was because she truly felt that way about Harvey or if it was just because she felt so good herself.

It was confusing not knowing.

Giorgio's was a indoor/outdoor restaurant neatly tucked into an area near the foot of one of the most spectacular bridges Sabrina had seen so far. Like the others she'd seen, it arched high over the bustling canal traffic below. Gondolas, *vaporettis,* and fishing boats made up most of the traffic. The breeze swirled through between the buildings only fast enough to barely ruffle the yellow and orange umbrellas over the white wrought-iron tables. All of them looked taken.

"Wow," Harvey said. "This is kind of a ritzy place."

"Yes," Sabrina said, staring at the line of prospective diners waiting to be seated. For a small place, Giorgio's did a lot of business.

"I always wished I could bring you to places like these," Harvey said, eyes gleaming as he watched the maitre d' standing near a podium.

"That's okay," Sabrina said. *I always had fun on the dates we went on, Harvey.* But she was suddenly shy about their past. After all, they'd both agreed to see other people.

Harvey shifted anxiously, staring at the line of people. "Well, we're not going to wait here."

"What?"

Harvey started forward purposefully. Sabrina tried to grab his arm, but missed.

"Hey!" Harvey yelled at the maitre d'. "Garkon!"

Garkon? Does he mean Garçon? Sabrina's cheeks flamed in embarrassment. If Harvey hadn't thought he was dreaming, he'd never have done something so outrageous.

The maitre d' glanced up in disbelieving annoyance.

"I've got five bucks here that says you can find us a table in the next two minutes." Harvey held the bill up, then looked over his shoulder and grinned at Sabrina. "For a minute there, I forgot this was a dream. Just watch."

Sabrina got hold of his arm and started pulling him away. "I think this is a really bad idea."

"No, it'll be okay."

The maitre d' snapped his fingers at a couple of broad-shouldered waiters. Sabrina figured she and Harvey were both about to end up in the canal. She pulled at his arm, actually managing to get him to take a couple of steps back.

The waiters closed in on them.

"Stefan!" A man's voice rang out loud and clear. "Vincenzo!"

Both the waiters froze in their tracks and looked back.

Sabrina stared between them, her attention fixed even though she felt she should be running.

An immaculate man in a crisp Armani suit stood in the double-doorway of Giorgio's. He was bald except for a black fringe that he kept slicked back. A delicate mustache colored his upper lip. "Please," he said, "don't trouble my guests. I have a reserved table waiting for them." He held out a hand and gestured. "Bring them inside."

Then Sabrina saw Salem in the man's arms and understood.

"Thanks, garkon," Harvey said, slapping the maitre d's shoulder and drawing the attention of all the diners and all those still standing in line.

Sabrina pulled on his arm before he could do anything else, then led him into the restaurant.

"You are a very pretty young lady," the bald man greeted. He captured Sabrina's free hand and briefly kissed it. "I am Giorgio La Mancha, and this morning I will be your host as you are friends of my good friend, Salem Saberhagen."

"Hey, that's just great, George," Harvey said, then tucked the five-dollar bill inside Giorgio's jacket pocket. He winked at Sabrina. "See? Told you it'd work."

Sabrina hurriedly said, "I'm Sabrina Spellman, and this is my friend, Harvey Kinkle. He's—uh—not exactly feeling himself this morning. Long trip, you know."

"Actually," Harvey objected, "it lasted maybe a minute or so. We just stepped into Sabrina's linen closet, then we were here faster than you can say, 'Beam me up, Scotty.'"

"How delightful for you," Giorgio said, ignoring Harvey's behavior with the ease born of years as a host. He removed the five-dollar bill from his jacket pocket and gave it back to Harvey. "Your money is no good here. As my guests, I'll see that you're well taken care of."

"Terrific," Harvey said. Sabrina pulled him along after the restaurant owner.

Salem peered at Harvey over Giorgio's shoulder. "You might want to tone it down in here. This is a classy place."

Harvey shrugged and continued looking around. He yawned, then apologized. "Never have been sleepy in a dream before."

"It's okay," Sabrina told him. "Let's enjoy breakfast. *Quietly.*"

"Sure."

Giorgio put them at a table near the front of the restaurant, pulling Sabrina's chair out himself. She sat down and gazed around at her surroundings.

The restaurant's elegance captured her attention. Flowers and beautiful wine bottles and flasks adorned the dining area. Fishing nets hung from the ceiling and draped some of the walls, holding more exotic glassware fixed so they could be easily observed. The colors ran the gamut from a light electric blue to a pale coral. Some of the long bottles had model ships inside. A small dance floor occupied the front of the restaurant beneath a colorful spray of balloons.

Salem sat in a chair across from Sabrina, daintily resting a paw on the embroidered cream-colored linen napkin. "Since I'm familiar with the menu," he purred, "maybe I could order for all of us."

"Sure," Harvey said, gazing at the proffered menu. "But it's strange how I seem to be able to speak and read Italian."

Sabrina nodded at Salem, then waited till the cat finished ordering. When Giorgio was free, she asked, "Is there going to be entertainment?"

"You're talking about the stage?" Giorgio asked.

"Yes."

Giorgio opened his hands and smiled. "Of a sort. We're providing a karaoke this morning. Everyone in the restaurant is invited to sing if they wish. Are you talented?"

"Not enough at singing." Sabrina grinned, enjoying the man's charm.

Giorgio smiled in return. "I'll go see to your meals."

Harvey stared at the stage, drumming his hands on the table in time to the lively background music that carried over the length of the restaurant.

Shaking his head, Salem said, "This really isn't turning out to be the quiet breakfast I thought you had in mind."

Sabrina silently agreed, but she wasn't going to give Salem the satisfaction of knowing that. "How do you know Giorgio?"

"We go back," Salem said. "He wasn't always a restaurant owner. He's also one of us." He blinked in Harvey's direction. "Is he going to be all right?"

"I think so."

"Well, watch him, because he almost cost us breakfast with that attitude."

The first course arrived. It was a pastry dish filled with fresh fruit, an amount small enough to only wake the palate rather than satisfy a true hunger. Salem told Sabrina the name of it, but she forgot it while watching the restaurant's clientele.

The karaoke contest got under way as well, and the first contestants were a three-woman group singing a '60s song. They were okay, Sabrina thought, but a little nervous. The next two contestants were even more so. They were followed by a college-aged guy in tight leather pants, an open shirt, and an attitude.

"Man," Harvey complained, "that guy wouldn't know how to carry a tune if it bit him on the nose."

Salem looked at him, then switched his gaze to Sabrina. "He's not going to make it. He's even losing his similes."

Sabrina had to admit that Harvey was looking sleepy. *Maybe we should just call it a night after breakfast.* She was reluctant to do that, though.

The bad luck was waiting for her back in Westbridge.

The karaoke contest continued.

Giorgio came back over as they were finishing the pastry. "Everything is acceptable?"

"But of course, my old friend," Salem said, smiling his biggest cat smile. "I told my companions we could only expect the best here."

Giorgio politely bowed his thanks. "I'm glad to hear you say that. Today is a most important day."

"How so?" Salem asked.

"Today," Giorgio announced proudly, "Giorgio's is being featured on the Exotic Vacations segment of *Rhys and Schine.*"

Sabrina recognized the name of the show. Phil Rhys and Rebecca Schine were two of the hottest talk show hosts on television. They'd only started their syndicated show a few months ago, but already a large number of people in Westbridge had tuned in to it. Including Aunt Zelda and Aunt Hilda.

"Rhys and Schine are here?" Salem repeated.

Giorgio nodded happily. "Not them. But the travel staff got here bright and early." He gestured to the right. "I gave them one of the best tables in the restaurant." He waved.

Glancing across the crowded room, Sabrina spotted Danny Martin, the talk show's host for the Exotic Vacations segment, waving back at Giorgio. Danny was young and cool, always dressed in cutting-edge style. His blond hair caught the lights.

"They're here reviewing the restaurant as part of their Venice show," Giorgio said. "I sponsored the karaoke contest as an added feature. But it should draw a lot of attention for the restaurant." He wandered away, called by one of the wait staff.

More attention than you realize, Sabrina admitted. She caught Salem's eye. "Maybe we should go."

"One of us," Salem said, "already has."

It took a moment for the cat's meaning to sink in. Sabrina glanced at Harvey's chair and found it empty. "Where is he?"

Salem rolled his shoulders in a cat-shrug. He sunk a claw into a juicy mango morsel. "He just got up and went. I figured he was looking for the bathroom." Tossing the mango bit into the air, he snapped it up as it fell, chewing in obvious satisfaction.

"We've got to find him," Sabrina said.

Spotting the second breakfast course coming their way, Salem said, "I'll wait here. In case he comes back."

Sabrina didn't waste time trying to argue. She left and worked her way through the tables. Harvey was nowhere to be found. Back in the hallway where the bathrooms were, she wondered how she was going to go into the men's room to check if Harvey was there.

A young guy came by in a denim shirt and khakis, but the white sneakers gave him away. *An American!* Working quickly, Sabrina zapped up a picture of Harvey, then said, "Excuse me."

The guy turned around. "Yes?"

For a moment Sabrina was distracted by the white smile and glint in his dark eyes. *Oh, wow!*

"May I help you?" the guy asked.

Sabrina chided herself for losing her train of thought. *Why do I have to be so interested in guys? Why can't I just be happy with Harvey like I want to?* She quickly zapped up a picture. "I'm looking for my friend. I think he may be in there sick. Could you check?"

The guy grinned and raked his dark hair out of his face with his fingers. "Oh, but he's not in there. He's in line for the karaoke."

"What?" Sabrina barely restrained herself from screaming.

The guy lost some of his confidence and some of his smile. He pointed back out into the restaurant. "He's in the karaoke line. He should be coming up soon."

Sabrina ran back out into the restaurant. Harvey was a good singer in his own right, and once she'd even gifted him with Elvis's voice, which had caused problems. And his normal reluctance to step into the spotlight wasn't going to be working because he thought he was just dreaming.

She arrived just in time to watch Harvey walk

out onto the stage. He accepted the microphone from the pretty hostess then turned to face the audience.

"Coming to you this morning from Giorgio's in Venice," the hostess said, "is American singing sensation, Harvey! He'll be performing a hit from the Monkees called 'I'm a Believer.'"

Sabrina couldn't believe what she was seeing as the spotlight tightened up and focused on Harvey. This was *television*. Everybody in Westbridge who was tuned in to *Rhys and Schine* was going to see Harvey Kinkle singing in Venice when he should have been home in bed!

Uh-oh, it's my bad luck! Sabrina knew it. The bad luck had even followed her here—and it was as bad as it could get.

Smiling and obviously feeling cocky, Harvey let the rock and roll music lead him, then opened up with the song. His voice thundered over the speakers as he launched into the refrain. His performance, Sabrina had to admit, was light years ahead of the other contestants. Part of it was natural talent and skill, but the other part was because he had no inhibitions about performing.

The audience joined in at the refrain, the voices sweeping through the restaurant, carrying Harvey's voice above them.

"I'm a believer, yeah, yeah, yeah . . ."

Sabrina watched in disbelief as Danny Martin's film crew spread out to film Harvey from all angles. Harvey used every inch of the stage, strutting and posing and enjoying himself like he was back in his room in front of a mirror instead of in a crowded restaurant. His innocence and enjoyment captured the room, winning them over.

Watching him, Sabrina felt entranced herself as he gave himself over to the vocals. But the other part of her was mortified. She rejoined Salem at their table.

"We are dead," Sabrina said as Harvey finished the song. "We are *so* dead."

"We?" Salem echoed, looking up from the plate in front of him. "I thought the deal was I wasn't going to take any heat for this little jaunt of yours."

"With Harvey appearing on *Rhys and Schine* do you really think Aunt Hilda and Aunt Zelda aren't going to notice?"

Salem swished his tail anxiously. "Well—no."

"Exactly."

He started whimpering. "I can't believe I let you talk me into this."

"Oh, quit!" Sabrina said impatiently. "As if you've never talked me into anything that got me into trouble."

"I did that out of the goodness of my heart. *Every*time."

Harvey's song finished, then Giorgio joined him up on stage. "Ladies and gentlemen," the restaurant owner said, "I think it's safe to say that we have our winner!"

A round of thunderous applause filled the dining area.

Reluctantly, Sabrina joined in. She couldn't believe breaking that mirror could result in this much bad luck. What explanation was she going to offer for Harvey being in Venice? Her aunts would understand the linen closet—even if they didn't approve—but none of the mortal world would. To zap him back and erase his memory was one thing, but how could she get to everyone who watched the show?

"Hey," Harvey said, smiling as he rejoined them at their table. People around them were still offering their congratulations. "Wasn't that great, Sab?"

"Yes," Sabrina said, watching the stage. Maybe it didn't have to be over. Maybe she could zap the next contestant and give them a performance that would bring the house down. *But that would be so unfair to Harvey. He worked hard and really deserves whatever prize he gets.*

Still, she couldn't allow the mortal world to know that witches actually existed either.

It was close to ten o'clock here, which meant it was still early back home. *How do I fix this? I can't turn back time . . .*

Up on stage, the hostess offered the microphone to the audience, but no one took it.

"I always dreamed of getting up on stage and doing that," Harvey admitted, stifling a yawn. "But then, I guess I'm still dreaming, right?"

"Right," Sabrina said. *What am I going to do?*
She thought furiously, but nothing came to mind.
Well, one thing did. She said a quick spell.

> *"Harvey sang well, and Harvey sang true,*
> *But his singing has got me blue.*
> *Now to get out of trouble deep,*
> *Put everyone in the restaurant except Salem*
> *and me to sleep."*

Instantly all the people in the restaurant went to
sleep.

"What are you going to do?" Salem asked. "Put
up a big thornbush and wake them in a hundred
years when all of the trouble has blown over?"

"I'm going to do the only thing I can," Sabrina
replied. "I'm going to the Witches' Council and
ask them to turn back time." Saying it out loud
didn't sound so good, though.

"Might I point out," Salem said, "that the
Witches' Council has already turned back time for
you once?"

"You're saying they won't do it again? Can't
you see how bad this is?"

"I'm saying that they're not going to be over-
joyed about it."

"Maybe there's another way," Sabrina said.
"Remember All-You-Can-Cast Day? About the
extra day that's given to witches every so often to
cast all the spells they want without repercus-
sions?"

"Yes . . ." Salem said slowly, licking his plate with his rough, pink tongue.

"So there must just be extra time laying around here. Where else could we get that whole extra day? All I have to do is erase the past ten minutes, get Harvey out of here before he decides to go up to the karaoke stage and *voila!*—no more problems."

"Someone will notice," Salem told her.

"No way. It's only ten minutes. Who notices ten minutes? Do you know how *short* ten minutes is?"

"The witches in the Chronal Flow Office will notice. And whatever time you turn back will be under review by the Witches' Council later."

That caught Sabrina's attention. "Nobody mentioned the Chronal Flow Office in the book of magic."

"Trust me," Salem said knowingly, "they're there."

"Surely the Witches' Council would agree turning back time is what needs to be done?"

"I don't know. They can be awfully sticky about details. Trust me."

"Then what should we do?"

Salem eyed the plate in front of him. "Congratulate Harvey and enjoy our last meal?"

Despite Salem's advice, Sabrina felt turning back time ten minutes was the only answer. When the Witches' Council turned back time, they could do so without causing any aftereffects in the time stream.

Right?

She felt frustrated and angry. *I didn't deserve all this bad luck. It's not fair.*

Sabrina wanted to scream. She stared out at all the people sleeping at the tables. *They have normal lives today. Why can't I?* The spell was on the tip of her tongue, one of the few she'd memorized. Who knew when ten minutes was going to come in handy?

How could a dream date with Harvey go so wrong?

Going under review by the Witches' Council wasn't something she was looking forward to either.

She looked out the window to the plaza, where a flock of pigeons rose suddenly and veered off into the sunlight, revealing two tourists standing at the entrance to Giorgio's sidewalk cafe. They were consulting the posted menu and their guidebook, while juggling a camera and a phrasebook. Then a stroke of brilliance struck her. She pointed at Danny Martin's film crew and mouthed a quick spell. Then she removed the sleep spell from the restaurant. She took Harvey by the hand and picked up Salem. "Gotta go."

"What about lunch?" Salem protested.

"I'll get you a doggie bag," Sabrina said.

Salem glared at her.

"Sorry," she said, then pointed up a bag that fit neatly between his teeth.

"Where are we going?" Harvey asked.

"Home. Dream's over." She waved to Giorgio and grabbed her backpack.

"Yeah, but Danny Martin is supposed to interview me for the television show. I may even get to sing another number."

"You're waking up. I can't control this. You're waking up in your own bed." Sabrina pulled them into an alley outside, then stepped around the corner. In the next instant, they were back in the linen closet in the Spellman home.

She zapped Harvey back into his pajamas, then back to his home.

Still anxious, Sabrina couldn't go back to sleep, so she camped out in the recliner in the living room. Salem contented himself with the remnants of the breakfast, then stretched out on the recliner's back above her.

"Sabrina?" Aunt Zelda called out. "You're up awfully early this morning."

Sabrina popped her eyes open with effort as her aunts approached. "I'm really excited about the day."

Zelda and Hilda seated themselves on the couch, then pointed up cups of coffee.

"And what an *interesting* outfit." Hilda noted. "Can I get you something to eat?"

"Hot chocolate would be good," Sabrina said. "I can get it myself."

"I'll do it. You don't look like you're fully awake."

In the next instant, a steaming mug of hot chocolate filled Sabrina's hand.

Zelda switched the television on, tuning in *Rhys and Schine*. "You know, these guys are so entertaining. I just love giving up my morning hour to them. I'm sorry I got up late."

"Coming to us live now from Venice, Italy," Rhys was saying, "is our very own Danny Martin."

Sabrina sat up straight so fast she almost dropped her mug. Her breath tightened in her throat. Had she managed to defeat her bad luck again, or was this the instance that was going to bring her down?

"I have to tell you," Danny Martin said, "Venice is really the place to be if you want to see true Old World charm. And you'll get double helpings of it—and everything else—at Giorgio's, a local restaurant with a flair for elegance. Giorgio even provided entertainment for our crew this morning."

The television camera focused on Danny Martin with the Palace of the Doges in the background, then segued into the interior of Giorgio's. The stage came into near focus, but the image of Harvey Kinkle was blurred a bit, making it hard to recognize him.

"What are we looking at here, Danny?" Rhys asked from his Boston studio.

"The winner of the karaoke contest," Danny answered. "I apologize for the quality of the tape.

We must have been having technical difficulties that we weren't aware of at the time. But this kid was great. Really knocked our socks off with his rendition of 'I'm A Believer,' by the Monkees."

The tape changed again, tightening up the focus on Harvey but still not quite getting rid of all the blurring. Then his voice came across, strong and rocking. Only it was all in Italian. No one would recognize it as belonging to Harvey Kinkle.

"It's strange," Danny said in a voice-over as Harvey continued to sing, "but at the time we were listening to him, I swear he sang in English. I understood every word."

Sabrina's spell had taken care of that too. *Yes!*

"Maybe it was just your familiarity with the song," Rhys suggested in his soothing, broadcaster voice. "Tell us more about your visit so far there in Venice."

Sabrina let out a sigh of relief. Her spell had worked, and her secret was safe. No one watching the show would recognize the karaoke singer as Harvey.

"You know," Zelda said, "that boy reminds me of Harvey." She turned her gaze on Sabrina.

"That's ridiculous," Sabrina said with a forced laugh. "What would *Harvey* be doing in Venice?"

"Karaoke, perhaps?" Zelda said.

"In Italian?"

"We could," Hilda suggested, lowering her eyebrows and looking suspicious herself, "check the linen closet. We *are* on the Frequent Witch Flyer

Program. Maybe we racked up some additional miles overnight that we don't know about . . ."

Zelda nodded, sitting back and crossing her arms.

"But I don't think we'll have to go quite that far." Hilda held up a white paper bag that had obviously been mauled by a cat. There, in green ink for everyone to see, was the name GIORGIO'S DI VENIZIA.

"I can explain," Sabrina said.

"Believe me," Zelda said, "you will. Starting now. Then we're going to talk about grounding."

"Bummer," Salem said. Then burped loudly. "Is there anything left in that bag?"

Hilda zapped it into nothing.

"I didn't think so." He stood and stretched. "I think I'll go up—"

"No, you won't," Hilda said. "As I recall, you and Giorgio are friends. Something to do with the flooding of Venice? Anyway, I don't think Sabrina went alone."

Salem switched his gaze onto Sabrina. "I *told* you I'd get blamed for this."

"It wasn't Salem's fault," Sabrina said. Then she started telling them the whole story. Throwing herself on the mercy of the court wasn't something she liked to do. But she started to relax. After all, no matter what her aunts said or did, she now knew the rest of the day was going to be without any more bad luck. There was a lot of the day left and she planned to make the most of it.

After all, they wouldn't ground her from school. Would they?

Nah, she thought as Zelda continued to list the things Sabrina was grounded from. *Being grounded from school would count as* good *luck!*

"Ah, dearie." The mirror sighed as another shard of glass settled into place. "That's molto bene! *Halfway there!"*

THURSDAY

Thursday's Child Works for a Living
By Mark Dubowski

"Take it from a black cat," Salem said. "There's no cure for bad luck."

"You mean I'm stuck with it—*forever?*" Sabrina worried aloud.

"It's more like catching a cold. Stay in bed, drink plenty of liquids, and watch a lot of TV."

Sabrina had just finished her orange juice. She showed him the empty glass. "I can't stay in bed though—I'm in charge of the Spirit Club. We have a major pep rally coming up."

"Not good!" Salem said, curling into a napping position on the counter. "You have to learn to take it easy, Sabrina. Like the song goes, 'Walk, don't run.'"

Sabrina looked out the window. It was a perfect day. Long shadows on the lawn, bright leaves on the trees against a spanking blue New England sky. "Hm. That's not a bad idea," she said.

"Walking, I mean. I think I'll walk to school today, instead of taking the bus. I think a change might do me good. Who knows, maybe bad luck won't know where I am." She grabbed her book bag and headed out the front door. "After all, I *am* past the halfway mark, right?"

"Good luck, kiddo." Salem said.

Sabrina walked the same streets the bus took every morning. But walking allowed her time to really notice things. The blue house she passed every morning, for example, had a beautiful garden behind its white picket fence. The Westbridge Drug Store smelled like wet pavement from where the druggist had cleaned the sidewalk with a hose. And another store Sabrina thought closed long ago had become offices of some kind. A sign in the window now advertised for part-time help:

HELP WANTED!
Temporary/Part-Time! Cash, Quick!
Good Luck Manufacturing Company

Curious, Sabrina stuck her head in the open doorway.

"Pretty lady!" a man inside exclaimed. "How about a fantastic part-time job? At Good Luck Manufacturing Company, every day is your lucky day!"

I wish, Sabrina thought.

The man came to the door with another person,

a woman, and stuck out his hand. They were Asian, a lot shorter than Sabrina, old, but vigorous-looking. "My name is Victor Won!" the man said with great enthusiasm. "Pleased to meet you!" They shook hands. He motioned toward his companion and introduced her as his wife, "Li, inventor of the Puzzle Baby." The woman smiled, then grinned broadly.

"Puzzle Babies. I've heard of those," Sabrina said. They were just ordinary plastic baby dolls, except they had a puzzled expression on their faces and came with a paper tag that had a riddle on it. You left the tag on; the idea was to accumulate dolls with different riddles. What Sabrina found puzzling was that people were actually collecting them. Some people were even willing to pay extra for the ones that had riddles that were especially funny. But she understood those were rare.

"You make your big fortune at Good Luck!" the lady promised Sabrina. She rubbed her thumb and index finger together, like she was feeling some money.

"No thanks," Sabrina said. "I've got a pretty busy schedule. I'm in high school and I'm kinda grounded at the moment." She smiled and went back outside.

"You could work after school!" Mr. Won called. He'd stepped out onto the sidewalk after her. "You even get paid the same day!"

"Maybe another day!" Sabrina called over her shoulder.

"At Good Luck Manufacturing Company, every day is your lucky day!" Mrs. Won reminded her.

At Westbridge High, it was Sabrina's unlucky day, however.

A few minutes before first period she ran into Harvey and Valerie at her locker. They'd been waiting for her. Harvey wanted to show Val the new prop the Spirit Club had made for the pep rally, and Sabrina had the key to the storage room.

"Come on, I'll go with you," Sabrina said.

Big mistake.

For weeks the Spirit Club had been working on a prop for the pep rally and upcoming football game. They'd kept everything top secret. The plan was to unveil it at the pep rally and bring it out again at the big game. It was a ten-foot-long scallion. A Fighting Scallion, the Westbridge school mascot. The original mascot was a stallion, but a mix-up at the printing plant had turned the word into *scallion,* and the name had stuck ever since.

"Oh, it's so cool!" Valerie gasped.

"Thank you," Harvey said with a crinkley smile. "I put the motor in."

"It's got a *motor?*" Valerie gasped.

"Isn't it great?" Sabrina said. "The Fighting Scallion bucks like a wild bronco when you turn it on. Look out Macy's parade, if you know what I mean."

"I'm impressed!" Valerie said. "Can you turn it on now for just a minute?"

"Oh, sure," Sabrina said. "No problem!"

Big mistake.

The minute Sabrina pushed the plug into the wall outlet, a scream and loud *bang!* went off deep inside the scallion. The smell of fried rubber filled the storage room.

A power surge had zapped the motor!

"Oh, no," Sabrina said. "The pep rally—"

Harvey crawled underneath the scallion to survey the damage. "This thing's toast," he told them.

Sabrina grimaced. "Me, too."

"Westbridge Electrical Supply to the rescue!" Harvey beamed. They were in Vice-principal Kraft's office. He'd let them use the phone to check on a new motor. The original one had come from the scrap-metal box in Harvey's dad's shop. Fortunately, the local supply house had a new one just like it in stock. "He's getting the price now," Harvey said.

"I hope it's not too expensive," Sabrina said, worried. As president of the Spirit Club, she was quite familiar with the club's budget. They didn't keep a lot of extra cash on hand for emergencies. This was a first.

"Hold on a minute," Harvey said, then covered the phone and talked to Sabrina. "It's only fifty bucks. They're letting us have it at their cost—no profit. Plus they'll deliver it free, first thing tomorrow morning. Should I go ahead and order it?"

Sabrina thought fast. She knew exactly how much they had in their treasury. Fifty dollars was about $47.50 more than they could afford.

"Do it," Sabrina said.

Harvey placed the order while Sabrina tried to deal with what she'd just done. *Where am I going to come up with $47.50?* She had less than twenty-four hours.

There wasn't time to hold a fund-raiser.

She'd spent her own savings the day before on that little fiasco in Venice.

She needed a new source of income, right away.

Surely she could figure out a way to earn $47.50.

Salem's words haunted her. "Good luck, kiddo."

That's it! Sabrina thought. The Good Luck Manufacturing Company! Didn't Mr. Won say she could work after school, anytime? Didn't he say she would get paid the same day? Didn't Mrs. Won say Sabrina would make a fortune? She didn't need that much. Only $47.50.

"It really is your lucky day!" Mrs. Won said.

"Welcome to the Good Luck team!" Mr. Won said.

Earlier, Sabrina had explained the whole situation to her aunts on the telephone. How the Fighting Scallion had burned out in the storage

144

room, that she needed to work after school to raise money for the new motor, where she would be, the address and phone number. For a couple of witches who had grounded her the day before, Hilda and Zelda were very understanding. "After all, it's for the school. And it'll look good on my college application." Sabrina played her trump card. They were even going to pick her up after work.

"Just give us a call when you've earned your $47.50," Hilda had said.

Now Mr. Won was promising Sabrina she'd have that much in no time. "I'll let you know when you have $47.50 coming," he promised.

Then he'd presented her with a Good Luck Manufacturing Company official employee uniform. It looked like the coveralls that factory workers wear.

That's because that's what it was. Good Luck Manufacturing had a small workshop in the back room where they made Puzzle Babies. Sabrina could hear the machines pounding them out as Mrs. Won led her down a hallway to a locker room where she could change. When she was ready, Mrs. Won sent her the rest of the way down the hall to where Mr. Won was waiting.

"You're gonna like it here," Mr. Won shouted above the clanking, hissing, and crashing noises in the factory. They stopped at a large black contraption that was leaking steam. A woman was pouring buckets of plastic beads in one end and a man was removing buckets of molten plastic from the other. "Puzzle Baby juice," Mr. Won explained.

From here the juice went into another machine that was being watched by a worker wearing a yellow hard hat. "This person is the head engineer," Mr. Won said about him. The man pulled a lever and the machine bucked and slammed. Several hundred tiny doll heads jiggled out into a metal bucket. Puzzle Baby heads.

The next machine turned juice into left arms. A machine across the aisle turned juice into right arms. There were two machines that made hands. Another two that made legs. Two for feet. It even took two machines to make the body, one for the left side and another for the right.

"From here, all the parts are put into a barrel and taken to the assembly table." The barrel was about the size of a washing machine. It was just now full. A man came and wheeled it away. Sabrina and Mr. Won followed him to the assembly table.

"This is where you work," Mr. Won shouted when they got there. Three people in uniforms like Sabrina's were seated at a large table. Mr. Won pulled out an empty chair for Sabrina. "You'll get the hang of it in no time! See you in two hours," he yelled, "at break time!" Then he left.

Sabrina watched the others to find out what she should do. First the man with the drum poured a

big avalanche of mixed-up Puzzle Baby parts onto the table. The three assembly-table workers
quickly divided it up into individual piles to pick
through and put together. The plastic pieces of the
doll made a popping noise as they snapped together. When a worker had completed a Puzzle
Baby, he tied on a small paper tag—the riddle—
and dropped the baby in a clear plastic bag that
snapped closed. Finally they stapled a cardboard
label on it and tossed the finished product with
others into large cardboard boxes.

Sabrina was amazed at how fast the assembly-
table workers were. Their hands flew through the
pieces. Sabrina figured they'd get through the pile
in no time. Then what would they do?

Right away the man with the drum came back
and poured another load onto the table.

Sabrina scraped an armload of parts over to her
spot and got to work.

This isn't hard, Sabrina thought after a few
minutes. *It's impossible!*

First of all, there were a lot of pieces. Why
wasn't the hand part of the arm already? Why did
it have to be in two pieces? Second, all the pieces
were mixed up. They came from different machines—why did the workers mix everything up
in one barrel before taking them to the assembly
table? It looked as if it was because they only *had*
one barrel.

And finally, why were the pieces made to be so
hard to put together? The left arm had to go in the

left arm hole, and the right arm in the right, of course. But except for the connector, the left arm and the right arm looked exactly the same. You had to think about it, and figure it out every time. The easy way was to just try to stick it in, and if it wouldn't go, you stuck it in the other side. The hands were like that, too. And the legs and the feet. It was crazy.

And Sabrina was convinced that it was making her co-workers crazy, too. She noticed the one man at her table who she thought was chewing gum try to blow a bubble and realized that he didn't have any gum. The blond woman sitting next to her whispered a karate scream every time she finished a doll, "Haieeeeee!" under her breath. And the woman across the table from her mumbled constantly.

How long could Sabrina hold on to her job? How long until the stress gave her strange habits? How long until she ran screaming from the building?

How long did Mr. Won say it would be until break time—two hours?

After a while Sabrina was no longer bothered by the noise from the machinery. She forgot all about it. Her hands hurt, but Mr. Won was right. She was getting faster—she was getting "the hang of it." The Puzzle Babies were kind of cute. Sabrina liked them. She liked Puzzle Babies. The Puzzle Babies were kind of cute. Sabrina liked them. She liked Puzzle Babies. The Puzzle Babies were kind of cute. Sabrina—

Buzzzzzzzzz! It was break time already!

Every machine in the building stopped at once. The silence was deafening. It hurt Sabrina's ears for it to be so quiet. Then people started talking. Everybody was smiling and chatting. Sabrina felt herself being swept along with the crowd of workers headed for the company break room. She knew then she would either have to quit or go mad.

Sabrina was halfway through writing her letter of resignation in her head when she came to the snack machines. Machines with clear plastic windows displayed bags of chips and bars of candy held in metal coils that were poised to let go at the drop of a coin. Machines with every kind of soda in hard, cold metal cans. Carousels of sandwiches. Sabrina was starving.

And broke.

"Need some money?" said a voice. It was the woman from across the table. The mumbler.

Sabrina almost said $47.50, but caught herself. "I could use a couple dollars, if you wouldn't mind lending me a little."

The woman took ten quarters out of her pocket and handed them over. "You have a good job, now," she said sweetly. "You'll have plenty of money now."

Sabrina felt like a rat. Now she owed this

woman $2.50. How could she even *think* about quitting? Surely she could stick it out for one day. She bought a sandwich, soda, and bag of chips and sat down at one of the tables with her new friend.

"Sabrina," Sabrina said, and held out her hand.

"Margaret," the woman said, giving it a shake.

"I don't know how you do it, Margaret," Sabrina said.

"Just get used to it, I guess," she said with a smile. "Did you forget about the noise?"

"From the machines? Yes! I did—how did you know?"

"Everybody forgets. Hands hurt?"

"Right!" It felt good knowing that someone else felt the same way.

"And you start talking to yourself inside your head. Over and over again."

"Exactly," Sabrina said. "I kept thinking 'Sabrina likes Puzzle Babies, Sabrina likes Puzzle Babies.'" She laughed.

"I know. I heard you."

"What?"

"Heard you."

"You *heard* me?" Sabrina didn't like *that*.

"Everybody heard you. You were saying it out loud."

"I was?" That really worried her.

"Everyone does it. I do it, too."

Sabrina remembered noticing this woman talk-

ing out loud. But not loud enough to understand.
"You say the same thing? Over and over?"

"Yes."

"What do you say?"

"It's my lucky day."

"It's your lucky day?" *Luck? Uh-oh!*

"It's my lucky day. It's my lucky day. It's my lucky day. It's my lucky day. It's my lucky day . . ."

Sabrina changed her mind. She was going to run screaming from the building after all. She was already getting out of her chair when Mr. Won came in.

"May I have your attention!" he ordered, loudly so everyone could hear. "I have a very important announcement to make!"

Sabrina sat back down.

"I have just received a very important phone call from a very big customer in New York!" Sabrina could hear the thrill in his voice.

He paused. A chair squeaked.

"The very big customer has made a decision!"

It was clear to Sabrina that everybody in the room knew what Mr. Won was talking about except her.

"The very big customer . . ."

Sabrina wished he would get on with it.

". . . has placed a *very* big order for Puzzle Babies!" A roar went up in the room, as if a war had ended. Mr. Won beamed. He clapped his hands along with everybody. The applause was deafening. It went on and on. But that was nothing compared to what happened next.

"And that means . . ." he said, "a very big raise for *you!*"

This time even Sabrina clapped.

After that Mr. Won thanked everyone for working hard. He explained that the big customer's order was very important. Eventually it would mean more jobs, and bigger and better machines. But right now, they had a tight deadline to meet. Everyone would have to pitch in and work extra hard. Make more Puzzle Babies. Twice as many as before.

Starting tonight.

The buzzer went off, signaling the end of break time, and workers evacuated the lunch room. Within seconds, the machinery was kicking and banging and spitting steam again. Caught up in the excitement, Sabrina found herself running for her place at the assembly table. The barrel man beat her—by the time she slid into her chair he had already dumped a load. It was going to be a wild night.

For the next fifty-nine minutes Sabrina worked feverishly to keep up with the others at her table. Body, head, arms, legs, hands, feet. Body, head, arms, legs, hands, feet. Body, head, arms, legs, hands, feet.

Never stopping. Never slowing down.

We'll never make it, Sabrina thought.

She knew the minute she spotted Margaret drop

an arm on the floor and reach into the pile to get another. That wasn't like Margaret.

Before, whenever Margaret dropped a Puzzle Baby part on the floor, she bent down to pick it up. She kept her work area neat. Spotless.

Another thing. The bubble gum man had stopped chewing. But he'd developed a blink. He was blinking his eyes, furiously, nonstop.

The woman who normally whispered karate screams hadn't changed except for the volume. Now each time she finished a doll she screamed for real.

The people in the factory weren't the only ones who were suffering under the new production schedule. Mr. and Mrs. Won were having a time of it, too. Their main job was coming up with riddles to go on the Puzzle Baby tags. Mrs. Won wrote them out by hand. Every now and then one or the other would walk down the hall and put in an appearance at the factory, and Sabrina could tell they'd been pulling on their hair.

The dolls weren't all coming out right, either. In their haste, the assembly-table people were all making mistakes, forcing the wrong parts together. Some of the dolls had legs coming out of their shoulders. Others had arms coming out of their hips.

Sabrina didn't want Mr. Won to lose his big customer, but she knew she had to do something before the people at the assembly table all had heart attacks. She was a witch, after all—she could fix this in a minute. She couldn't cast a spell on the machines that would slow everything down because then they would lose the customer's order. But she could cast a spell on the people at her table and speed them up. Or she could cast a spell on the table—it could help. Or she could cast a spell on some of the dolls, and they could put other dolls together.

That would be cool, Sabrina thought. But it was risky. Dolls sometimes behaved strangely while under a spell. Once in awhile they tried to take over, and that could be real trouble. Sabrina remembered her brief stint as a doll, thanks to her bratty cousin Amanda. The change of clothes was nice, but between the no-blinking and the arched feet, it was enough to drive a doll mad! The safe thing was to cast a spell on the people.

The magic words were just about to leave her lips when the Puzzle Baby doll in her hand did something strange.

It spoke!

"That's a no-no, Sabrina," the little doll said.

"No-no?"

"Definitely a no-no."

Sabrina gasped. "I didn't know you could talk!"

The doll smiled weirdly. Something about it seemed familiar. The face. It looked so familiar.

As a matter of fact, it looked like the *Quizmaster's* face.

As a matter of fact it *was* the Quizmaster's face!

Sabrina wasn't sure if the Quizmaster had

turned into a Puzzle Baby or a Puzzle Baby had turned into the Quizmaster. Either way, it was bad combination.

The riddle on its tag wasn't very good either— one of those chicken-crossing-the-road jokes.

The Quizmaster-face doll winked and *poof!*— the rest of it changed, too. Now it was all Quizmaster, except tiny. There he stood on the palm of Sabrina's hand, with his own hands on his hips, smiling broadly. He looked like he was really enjoying himself.

"Of course I can talk," he said. "And I can also catch you casting a spell when you're not supposed to, you little half-witch!"

In order to become a full witch, Sabrina had to abide by the rules of the Witches' Council. The Quizmaster was in charge of testing her. He knew that her week of bad luck would tempt her to break the rules. The council wanted to see that Sabrina had the self-discipline required to handle magic responsibly.

The Quizmaster was very big on self-discipline. He was extremely self-disciplined himself, and liked to prove it by doing things like eating just one potato chip. Sabrina thought he was excessive.

"Look who's calling who little," Sabrina said.

The Quizmaster snapped his fingers, freezing everything in the factory except Sabrina and himself. Then he jumped from her palm and enlarged to normal size. His green silk pants billowed around him. "You mean look who's calling *whom* little," the Quizmaster said. "But I'm not here to correct your grammar."

"Oh, I know," Sabrina said brightly. "You're here to loan me $47.50! I need it right away, and I promise I'll pay you back."

"No, that's not it, either," the Quizmaster told her. "The real reason I'm here is to remind you that casting a spell on mortals at this time would not be advisable. This whole day has been another test of your worthiness to become a full witch!"

"You don't understand," Sabrina said. "I have to do something—the machines are killing us. There's just no way the assembly people can keep up."

"Oh, you can do *something,* all right, Sabrina," the Quizmaster said. "You just can't use magic. Check your Witch's Handbook; it is forbidden to practice magic that will change people's mortal lives."

"I was thinking of *saving* their mortal lives. Human beings were not designed to work this fast."

The Quizmaster smiled and shook his head. "Think about it, Sabrina. If your magic makes them capable of producing Puzzle Babies faster than humanly possible, then what will happen tomorrow? Mr. Won will promise his customers even more. Where will it end? The Puzzle Baby people will become dependent on magic. That will never do!"

"Maybe I should just quit . . ." Sabrina thought out loud.

"And let your friends, and the Spirit Club, and the *whole school* down? I'd hate for you to have explain yourself at the pep rally. Nobody likes a bad onion, Sabrina."

"It's a scallion. Call it a scallion."

"Whatever. Anyway, I'm sure you'll think of something, Sabrina. Tootle-oo."

"Come back here!" Sabrina shouted. But it was too late. Puzzle Baby pieces spilled from the barrel into the already gigantic mound on the table in front of her as the Quizmaster vanished, unfreezing the factory. The half-finished Puzzle Baby she'd been working on reappeared in her hand.

"*Arrghhhhh!*" Sabrina growled. She felt like throwing the unassembled doll across the room. Instead, she just threw all the pieces in a bag the way they were and snapped it shut.

Which gave her a great idea.

"Mr. Won!" Sabrina yelled, bursting into his office. "I've got a great idea!"

Mr. Won was slumped in his chair, looking like he'd just completed the Boston Marathon. Mrs. Won was asleep on the floor. Actually they'd just completed the riddle tags for all the Puzzle Babies for the big customer's order. They were in a pile on his table—a few thousand, it looked like to Sabrina.

That's how many more dolls he was planning for them to make—that night!

"Go," he croaked, "back . . . to . . . work. Must . . . finish . . . assembling."

"We'll never finish!" Sabrina said, pointing at the tags. "It's humanly impossible."

"Nothing . . . is . . . impossible," said Mr. Won. He glanced at the wall. The words he'd just spoken were engraved on a plaque hanging there. Then he turned to his wife, lying still on the carpet. She looked dead. He looked back at Sabrina and said, "What . . . is . . . your . . . idea?"

Sabrina held up the bag she'd just finished. "This!"

Weakly, Mr. Won took the bag from her hand. He squinted and lines formed between his eyebrows. "It's not ready. Puzzle Baby is . . . no assembly required."

"No, Mr. Won, it's a puzzle! Get it? A Puzzle Baby *puzzle*. You buy it this way and put it together yourself!"

"Ahhhhh . . ." he said.

Was he saying he understood, or was he having a heart attack? Sabrina wasn't sure. Then the man's eyes brightened and a smile spread across his lips.

"Great idea . . ." he moaned.

Everybody in the factory liked the idea, too. Not only did they finish the work, they even got off early. Sabrina was a hero.

Even better, her job had been eliminated. Sabrina's idea made the assembly table so much more efficient that only three people were needed now.

Sabrina's pay for the four hours she'd worked was $50. But the Good Luck Manufacturing Company made its employees buy their uniforms, and they cost $50.

"But I told you every day at the Good Luck Manufacturing Company was your lucky day," Mrs. Won reminded Sabrina. "You still get $50. That's your bonus! For coming up with the Puzzle Baby Puzzle idea." The Wons presented her with $50 in cash.

Sabrina felt much better. The giant motorized Fighting Scallion would ride again! Plus her bonus came to $2.50, more than she needed to buy the new motor and just enough to pay Margaret back the money she'd borrowed to buy supper. Now that was lucky.

Best of all, the day was over. Hilda was coming to take her home.

Sabrina's back luck was behind her for now.

She'd passed another test of bad luck.

Five down, two to go. Whoo-hoo!

The mirror trembled slightly as another shard of broken glass settled into place. "Oh dear, so close. I hope she can pass the next test. So many witches have gotten this close and failed." Her one eye looked all around. "This time there will be too many people involved for a quick fix! Oh, dear. . . ."

Even before her job had been eliminated, Samantha had made the assembly table so much more
efficient that only three people were needed now.
Samantha made the four looms she'd worked
was $50. But the Good Luck Manufacturing
Company made its employees buy their uniforms
and they cost $40.

"But I told you every day at the Good Luck
Manufacturing Company was your lucky day!"
Mrs. Wen reminded Sabrina. "You still get $50.
That's your bonus! For coming up with the Puzzle
Baby Puzzle idea." Mrs. Wen presented her with
$50 in cash.

Sabrina felt much better. The giant motorized
Fighting Stallion would ride again! Now her bonus came to $2,50, more than she needed to buy
the new motor and just enough to pay Margaret
back the money she'd borrowed to buy supper.
Now that was lucky.

Best of all, the day was over. Eliza was coming
to take her home.

Sabrina's bad luck was behind her for now.
She'd passed another test of bad luck.
She'd survived another test.

The motor rumbled, digging at another shard of
broken glass, settled into place. "Oh, dear, no more. I
hope she can stay the next test. So many, so very
have gotten that done and failed." Her anxiety
locked off around. "This time there will be too
many people involved that a pack of Oh, dear."

FRIDAY

The Play's the Thing
By Cathy East Dubowski

Sunlight streamed in through Sabrina's stained-glass bedroom window, bathing her sleeping face in a rainbow of colors as she floated four feet above her bed.

Sabrina's nose twitched. She cracked one eye.

Morning . . .

Instantly the events of yesterday—and the days before that—filled her mind.

She groaned as she plunged through the air and landed with a *thump!* on her bed. "It was all a bad dream . . . a nightmare, right?"

"Wrong," Salem replied cattily, which was the tone of voice he probably would have used anyway even if he wasn't a warlock who'd been turned into a sleek black American shorthair by the Witches' Council.

Her wrists ached from . . . assembling Puzzle Babies! Then it was true—all of it. She buried her head under her pillow. "Won't this week ever end?" she mumbled.

Salem stretched lazily in the morning sun. "Of course," he purred. "But I'm not sure you'll still be in one piece when it does."

"Thanks a lot," Sabrina replied. "Better be nice to me. Or I might just decide that all my bad luck is caused by a certain black cat crossing my path!"

"Sabrina!" Salem exclaimed, jumping to his paws. "How dare you repeat such a ridiculously outdated superstition!"

"Hey, who says superstitions are ridiculous?"

"I do," Salem replied. "Besides, you know, of course, that in England it's the *white* cats that are bad luck," Salem reminded her. "But you know those crazy Colonials! Whatever the English did, they had to do the opposite. Coffee instead of tea. Black cats instead of white." Salem shivered. "Their stubbornness has *not* made my current incarnation in the States easy to live with."

"Well, I don't really believe in silly superstitions," Sabrina said, then quickly rapped her knuckles on her bedside table. "Knock on wood."

Maybe she could just stay in bed today. The week had already brought her failed interviews, a twisted ankle, lost bylines, mistaken identity, a jealous fit, a lost love, and sore wrists. How much bad luck could she have if she stayed hidden under the covers? But she knew she couldn't do that. Aunt Zelda would never allow her to skip school for anything less than a catastrophe. And besides, they had final rehearsal this afternoon for the drama club's production of *A Christmas Carol,* an adaptation of the book by Charles Dickens.

Sabrina jumped out of bed. With a quick snap of her fingers, she turned her long white nightgown into a white velvet T-shirt over black jeans. She covered her tootsies with black leather ankle boots. Then she grabbed her shoulder bag and zapped it full of her day's necessities—lip gloss, hairbrush, and a four-leaf-clover key ring for good luck.

But she had a sinking feeling it wouldn't help much.

Bad luck was out there waiting for her—who knew when she'd run into it?

She stuck her head out through the doorway into the hall and looked both ways.

Maybe if she was just really, really careful, she could spot bad luck coming—and outrun it. She shrugged. It was worth a try.

She tiptoed quickly across the ancient Persian hall runner and dashed down the front stairs.

So far, so good.

In the Spellmans' living room, Aunt Zelda sat sipping tea from one of her favorite antique teacups—the one that Shakespeare had given her for her birthday one year, along with that poem about "Shall I compare thee to a summer day?" Aunt Zelda usually didn't fall for literary types, but she'd confessed to Sabrina that she'd had quite a crush on the playwright. This morning, however, she seemed lost in her science journals.

Aunt Hilda had her nose glued to the TV set watching *Rhys and Schine* as a syrup bottle hovered in the air, pouring itself onto the plate of French toast Hilda balanced on her lap.

Sabrina tried to sneak out the front door.

"Sabrina . . ." Aunt Zelda called out without even glancing up.

That woman's got eyes in the back of her head! Sabrina grumbled to herself.

"Your brain cells can't go to school without a good breakfast."

Sabrina rolled her eyes. To please her aunt, she zapped a box of Dinky Donuts onto the hall table, stuck a chocolate one in her mouth, and grabbed a spare for the road. Witches couldn't do brand names, but these weren't half bad.

Now Zelda did turn and stare. "Sabrina! That's *not* a very nourishing breakfast!"

"Don't worry." Sabrina waved her hand, showering the doughnuts with multicolored sparkles. "Check the nutritional info on the side of the box. I fortified them with tofu extract, broccoli sprouts, and eight essential vitamins and minerals."

"Ewww!" Hilda gushed.

"But, Sabrina—" Zelda began.

"Gotta go!" Sabrina said quickly and dashed out the door before they could stop her and make her eat something with bran.

All morning long she kept an eye out for bad luck. But it didn't seem to have followed her to school that day. In fact, she didn't even see Vice-principal Kraft all day long. *Hey, things are looking up. Maybe the bad luck is wearing off.* It was near the end of the week, after all.

By the time the final bell rang, she was finally beginning to relax. She was really looking forward to tonight's performance. She'd been cast as the Ghost of Christmas Past—the ghost that carried Scrooge back into his past and showed him how happy his life used to be. Harvey was Bob Cratchit. Libby was Mrs. Cratchit. And Valerie was Tiny Tim.

"Okay, kids!" Mr. Pruitt, the student teacher who was acting as adviser for the play, called from the audience. "Let's get started. We don't have much time."

Just then Mrs. Quick, the math teacher, stuck her head in the door to the auditorium. "Mr. Pruitt, would you mind helping me for a moment? I have a filing cabinet I need to move."

"Of course." He stood up and called to the cast, "Go ahead and start without me. I'll be right back." Then he hurried down the hall with Mrs. Quick.

Sabrina dashed toward the wings, with her script in hand, rereading her opening lines for good luck.

"Sabrina!" Valerie shouted. "Look out! Don't walk under that ladder! It's—"

Sabrina looked up and realized she was directly under a ladder, Lloyd Krumley stood on which putting the final touches on a piece of scenery.

Sabrina tried to back out, but bumped the ladder.

Which jostled Lloyd—not known as Mr. Graceful to begin with.

He fell, grabbing the curtain . . .

Which ripped, causing Lloyd to lose his balance and drop his bucket of red paint . . .

Which splattered all over the set, the stage, her friend Valerie . . .

And the just-pressed costumes she was carrying toward the dressing rooms . . .

And, last but not least, all over Libby Chessler, who stood center stage practicing her bow.

Libby rose from her bow with red paint dripping down through her long dark hair.

Sabrina braced for the screams. But, except for Libby's "Ewwwwwwwww!" there was silence.

Total silence.

"Bad luck," Valerie said lamely.

The entire cast and crew of the Westbridge High School production of *A Christmas Carol* stared in stunned horror at their ruined set, stage, and costumes.

And the girl who had ruined them.

"Oops?" Sabrina squeaked.

Libby stormed over. With great drama, she wiped some of the red paint out of her hair and smeared it across Sabrina's white velvet T-shirt.

"Hey—"

"Way to go, *freak!*" Libby growled.

Okay. I'm convinced, Sabrina thought wryly. *The preceding scientific experiment has proved once and for all: Walking under a ladder is really bad luck!*

Now all her friends began talking at once.

"It's just a little paint," Sabrina said over the noise. "I'm sure we can clean it up. Why, there's a whole"—she glanced at her watch and gulped—*"three* hours to go till curtain time."

But no one seemed to be in the mood to listen to her.

And only Harvey said, "Sabrina, are you all right?"

Sabrina felt like crying. "Nope," she said.

She had to do something—quick! She raised her forefinger and stretched it, warming it up, trying to come up with some kind of spell, when . . .

She heard an odd buzzing sound.

Sabrina swatted around her ear.

The buzz seemed to say, *"Insta-Magic . . ."*

Sabrina glanced around. "Who said that?"

But no one was there.

Sabrina shrugged and started toward the janitor's closet to get something to clean up with.

"Insta-Magic . . ."

Sabrina frowned and planted her fists on her hips as she looked around.

No one. In fact, most of her schoolmates were staying far away from her. She couldn't blame them.

"Insta-Magic . . ."

There it was again!

And the strangest thing was . . . *It sounds like me!*

Hmm. Could it be her inner voice? Aunt Zelda always told her to listen to the "inner voice" deep within her for the answer to tough questions.

She'd always thought her inner voice was like her conscience—all the things she'd learned about right and wrong coming together to help her decide what to do in tough situations.

"Insta-Magic . . ." the voice whispered again. *"Wipe their minds . . ."*

Hey, it does sound like my voice, Sabrina thought. Maybe she should have paid more attention to Aunt Zelda's words. Maybe there was more to a witch's inner voice. Maybe it was like a sixth sense a witch could use. Sabrina hadn't known she was a witch all that long—only since the day she turned sixteen. And she was still a witch in training. She was learning new stuff about being a witch every day.

Maybe this inner voice could really give her advice—like an internal Dear Abby! *Hey, why else would it sound like me?* she thought.

"Insta Magic . . ."

170

It was tempting. With Insta-Magic she could simply and quickly clean up the entire mess she'd made.

Of course, there was one catch to that. Everyone would know that Sabrina was a witch.

But then she could make everyone forget what had happened. Wipe their minds as easily as using an eraser to clean the words from a chalkboard. Everything would be back to normal—and no one would remember anything that she did.

Perfect solution, right?

Wrong. Her aunts said it was a bad habit for a witch to clean up and worm her way out of a problem using magic.

But what good is magic if I can't use it to fix things? she thought.

"Exactly," the voice agreed.

Hey! It heard her—even though she hadn't spoken aloud! She rubbed her head. It *must* be in her own mind.

"Go ahead," the voice coaxed.

Besides, Sabrina thought, *this isn't for my own personal gain, right? This is to help others.*

Sabrina looked at the stage. Her friends—and Libby—had all turned toward her with shock and anger in their eyes.

Even Harvey and Valerie looked disappointed. She felt like a real Scrooge for ruining everything.

"Insta-Magic . . ."

"All right, all ready!" she snapped back at her inner voice.

Sabrina spread her feet and took a concentrated stance. She waved her arm dramatically.

"Quit with the David Copperfield dramatics and get on with it!" her inner voice nagged.

Sabrina rolled her eyes, then whispered a spell:

*"All this paint, all this mess,
Remove yourself from stage and dress!"*

Like a video running backward, the paint unspilled from the floor of the stage, Libby's hair, Valerie's armful of costumes, and Sabrina's white velvet T-shirt. Lloyd Krumley leaped backward and back up onto the ladder as his hand seemed to wipe away the tear in the curtain.

The fallen paint can slurped up all the red paint and then hopped back into Lloyd's hand.

Right after the accident, everyone had looked shocked.

Now they looked totally blown away.

Valerie stared at Sabrina, her expression a mixture of fright and delight. "I'm probably having a major teen mental breakdown. I mean, I'm sure I am. But it would be *so cool* if my best friend were really doing this."

Harvey looked as if you'd asked him the answer to a really hard math question.

Libby's eyes bulged as she realized that the freak she picked on every day seemed to possess some kind of special powers—powers that Sabrina might aim Libby's way.

Sabrina couldn't help but enjoy that for a moment—seeing Libby squirm.

And she couldn't help but think: *Wouldn't it be nice, at last, to tell everyone that I'm half mortal and half witch?*

But she quickly spurned that temptation. It could make life miserable for her aunts, and they'd been so good to her. She couldn't do anything to ruin the lives they'd made for themselves here.

"Don't forget to erase," her inner voice prompted.

"Oh, yeah—thanks," she whispered back. She'd better hurry, too, before Libby went screaming off to whine to Vice-principal Kraft.

Quickly she moved to Part Two of "Operation: Bad-Luck Cleanup":

> *"My hand's an eraser,*
> *I wave past your brow*
> *And erase all your memories*
> *Of the play up till now."*

It was not one of her more eloquent spells, but time was short. It would have to do.

Did it work?

The kids stopped staring at her. Tense brows relaxed as their expressions of shock and fear melted away. Instead, a look of pure happiness— almost goofy joy—spread across everyone's face.

Whew! Sabrina brushed her hands in front of her. *Job well done.*

Everything back to normal.

Sabrina smiled as the scene on stage picked up where it had left off, as if there'd been only a brief intermission.

Lloyd continued putting the finishing touches on a piece of scenery.

Valerie hurried backstage with an armful of costumes.

And Harvey and Libby resumed their position on stage to continue the rehearsal.

Libby smiled at Harvey and opened her mouth to say her line.

And her mouth hung open, gaping like a fish out of water.

No sound came out.

Libby cleared her throat. Embarrassed, she glanced around the stage, smiling, then tried again.

No sound came out.

Blushing—Sabrina didn't realize the girl knew how—Libby finally said, "Line!"

The stage manager glanced down at his script and read the first words of her next line: "Mr. Scrooge?"

Libby nodded, then opened her mouth. "Mr. Scrooge? Thuh . . ." She frowned in confusion, then stamped her foot. She shaded her eyes with her hand and glared up at the lighting crew. "Turn that stupid spotlight down! It's making me forget my lines!"

That's weird, Sabrina thought. Libby never forgot her lines.

The stage manager read her the entire line. "Mr. Scrooge? That stingy old man?"

Libby listened carefully, then repeated the entire line. She smiled a self-satisfied smile and turned to Harvey.

"I . . . uh." He frowned and glanced sideways.

Huh? Harvey was a little on the shy side, true. But like many shy people, he actually did well in front of an audience when he didn't have to think up what to say and could just lean on rehearsed lines. So he rarely forgot a line, either.

"Come on, Harvey," Sabrina whispered.

With an embarrassed shrug, Harvey mumbled, "Line."

The stage manager scratched his head and read the first few words of the next line. "Well, it is Christmas Day . . ."

"Thanks." Harvey took a deep breath. "Well, it is Christmas Day . . ."

Then stopped. Harvey sighed and shook his head. "I'm sorry, guys," he said, embarrassed. "I just can't seem to remember my lines today."

"Never mind!" Libby said. She opened her mouth to go on with her next line. But nothing came out. "Shoot!" she complained. "Line!"

Sabrina glanced at the stage manager. He stared back at Sabrina and shrugged.

Valerie, who was playing Tiny Tim, suddenly gasped, "I—I can't remember *my* lines!"

Then Libby's friend Cee Cee, who was playing the role of the Ghost of Christmas Future, whined nervously from the wings, "Hey, I can't remember my lines, either!"

Sabrina rolled her eyes. "Cee Cee, you don't *have* any lines!"

The Ghost of Christmas Future didn't speak in the play. It was just a dark, eerie ghost that floated around in its black robes and pointed at things, like Scrooge's tombstone.

Cee Cee had forgotten that she didn't have any lines to forget!

"Stop it, everybody!" Libby cried. "You're making me mess up!"

"No, we're not," Cee Cee replied. "You started it, Libby. You got us all nervous and shook up." The girl glanced around at the others for support. "Now none of us can remember our lines!"

This is way too weird, Sabrina thought. Everybody got stage fright before a play. Lots of people had dreams about forgetting their lines. But for everybody to totally forget all their lines at once?

Sabrina gulped. *Oh, no. It couldn't be. Don't tell me!* she told herself.

Ooops! said her inner voice. *Could it be you erased a little too much from their minds? Like maybe . . . all their lines?*

"Oh, no!" Sabrina cried. "This is *so* not cool!"

Especially since the play opened in just a few hours!

But a quick check of everyone on stage made it clear—Sabrina's spell to erase their memories of her magic cleanup had erased every single syllable of the play from their minds. Her spell rang in her ears. "Erase all your memories of the play up till now."

Now what am I going to do?

The Witches' Council would never grant her another time reversal. No way. They'd done that once—on her first day of school in Westbridge, the day she first found out she was a witch. But that was a once-in-a-lifetime happening, and she knew better than to even ask.

Maybe I can help them relearn their lines—real quick! she thought. She grabbed the script from the stage manager's hand and quickly flipped to the opening page. But even as she did, her heart sank. The script was something like a hundred pages long. No way could the cast learn it from scratch in less than three hours!

Sabrina glanced down at her silky robes. Her costume for the fairy-like Ghost of Christmas Past.

Hmmm . . . In the play the Ghost of Christmas Past led Scrooge back into his past to help him remember what his life had been like during the happier times of his youth.

Maybe she could do the same with her friends: take them back into their past—their recent past—to help them remember their lines!

Of course, she couldn't really take them back through time. But maybe through her magic, she could help them experience their past, much the same way psychiatrists helped their patients remember things from their childhood.

"Come here, everybody!" she shouted, calling the cast together in the center of the stage. "I've got an idea."

"We don't need your freak ideas, Sabrina," Libby said coolly.

"Oh, really?" Sabrina said, folding her arms. "Then I guess that means you have a better one?"

Libby opened her mouth. Then snapped it shut when nothing came out.

Sabrina liked the concept: Libby at a loss for words.

"Go ahead, then," Libby said through gritted teeth.

Sabrina faced the kids. "Hypnosis."

"You mean, like trances?" Harvey said. "Hey, cool!"

"I didn't know you knew how to do hypnosis," Valerie said. "Where did you learn that?"

"Um, uh—summer camp!" Sabrina fibbed. "You know, just goofing off around the campfire."

"Oh, I don't know," Lloyd said nervously. "I don't want anybody messing around with my mind."

"Yeah," said Libby. "You're not going to make us quack like a duck or anything just so you can make fun of us, are you?"

"No," Sabrina said, although the thought of turning Libby into a *real* waddling duck was tempting.

But there was no time for fun now, Sabrina told herself. She had work to do. Magic work. She'd need all the concentration she could muster to work a crowd this size.

"Don't worry," Sabrina said. "Hypnosis doesn't put you into a real trance. It's really just a heightened state of mental concentration. I'm not sure it will work on you, Libby," she couldn't resist saying, "but it's worth a try."

"I'm game," Harvey said affably.

Good old Harvey. "Thanks," Sabrina said with a smile. "If we're lucky, all your lines should come rushing back to your memory."

All of the kids—including Libby, reluctantly—agreed to try. Nobody wanted to face the curtain going up without knowing their lines.

Sabrina slipped off the golden locket she was wearing as part of her costume and held it in front of her.

"Okay, everybody, gather round."

Everyone squished in real close—like elevator close.

"Okay, not that close." Sabrina stepped back. Then she held the locket up and began to gently swing it.

Of course, the hypnosis she was going to use on her friends was a special kind—enhanced by her magic powers.

Slowly, slowly, her friends slipped into a relaxed hypnotic state—with a big boost from a little magic.

"I am the Ghost of Christmas Past," Sabrina said.

She'd never really taken anybody back into the past in their minds before, but if a ghost could do it, why not a witch?

"Relax your minds,
Float back in time,
Relive the play . . .
Of Christmas time."

There, that rhymed. But whoa, she was really turning out some clunkers today.

"I didn't know they used lame poems in hypnosis," Libby muttered, yawning.

"Shhh!" Sabrina said, then continued.

She had to hurry. Mr. Pruitt was sure to be back soon.

"Now, I'm going to count backward from ten to one," Sabrina said softly. "And when we reach the number one, you will open your eyes—and as an added bonus, you'll feel relaxed and refreshed."

Slowly she began to count backward from ten. ". . . three, two, . . . one."

The cast of *A Christmas Carol* opened their eyes. Everyone looked happy. That was a good sign. Everyone but Libby, that is.

With a pout, she ran up to Sabrina. "Pretty

necklace!" she said in a babyish voice. "I want it. Mine!" And with that, she snatched it from Sabrina's hands.

Whoa! What's that all about?

"I'm a pretty lady," Libby said as she put the necklace around her neck.

Before Sabrina could respond, Lloyd Krumley started making airplane noises and flying around the stage with his arms outstretched.

Cee Cee and Jill began playing with a doll they found in the prop bin.

Valerie looked at Sabrina with tears in her eyes. "Have you seen my mommy?"

Sabrina shook her head.

"I wanna go home!" Val wailed. Then she sat down on the edge of the stage and stuck her thumb in her mouth.

Before Sabrina could say a word, Harvey came up to her and yanked on her sleeve.

"Harvey—"

"What are you getting for Christmas?" he said in a little boy voice. "I asked Santa Claus for a pony, but I don't know if I'll get it. I've been pretty good. But my friend Eddie said that wasn't the real Santa at the mall—it was just one of his helpers. What do you think?"

"I think . . ." Sabrina didn't know what to think. "I'm sure you'll get it," she said at last.

"Really?"

"Really."

Harvey clapped his hands and wandered off to

where several of the boys were fooling around with Tiny Tim's crutch.

"I'm getting a Melinda Sue doll," Libby bragged. "It costs ninety hundred dollars!"

"Good for you," Sabrina muttered as she sat down at the Cratchits' humble kitchen table. "Now, run along, little girl. I've got work to do."

Libby stuck out her tongue. "That's what my daddy always says." Then she ran away to show off to Cee Cee and Jill.

I took them back into their past, all right! Sabrina thought. *Way back!* The cast and crew of *A Christmas Carol* were all children! She'd taken them back to the *play* of Christmastime when they were about five! Not the play *about* Christmas. *Oh, no!*

And in about two hours, their families, teachers, and friends would be sitting out in that audience expecting to see a play put on by well-rehearsed teenagers. If Sabrina didn't do something fast, they'd be watching *A Romp Through Mother Goose Land* instead.

Now what am I going to do?

"Insta-Magic . . ." her inner voice crooned.

"Oh, shut up!" Sabrina cried, leaping to her feet.

Around the stage several very grown-up looking children stared at her.

"Wahhhh!" cried Valerie. "She said shut up!"

"Shut up yourself!" Libby said, planting her

fists on her hips. "And I'm going to tell my mommy on you!"

Sabrina spotted her locket hanging around Libby's neck and sighed. There was only one thing to do. Try the hypnosis again, only this time try to get them to the right place in their memories.

"Libby, I need my necklace back," Sabrina said.

Libby grabbed it. "Uh-uh."

"Libby . . ."

Libby backed up. "No! You can't have it!"

Sabrina stepped toward her, and Libby began to run.

Sabrina ran after her. "Libby! Come back here!"

"Helllp!" Libby screamed.

Mr. Pruitt chose that moment to walk back into the auditorium. "What's going on?" he called from the doors at the back of the audience.

Sabrina froze. Uh-oh! She'd never be able to fix things with Mr. Pruitt watching. "Uh, we're just, um . . . doing a little improvisation. You know, to loosen up before the play."

"Ah! Excellent!" Mr. Pruitt said. He sat down in one of the seats. "Go ahead."

Sabrina grinned nervously. She glanced around the stage. Valerie was still sucking her thumb. Harvey and some of the other kids were running in and out of the wings playing tag. And now Libby was showing off to her friends how she could play "Jingle Bells" on the piano. Ouch! Very badly was how!

"Uh, Mr. Pruitt?" Sabrina called out into the audience. She crossed her fingers behind her back. "Mr. Kraft was just here. He said if we saw you, we should tell you to come by the office."

Mr. Pruitt leaped to his feet. "I'll be right back. Uh—proceed, students. You're doing great!"

As soon as he was gone, Sabrina shot a quick spell down the hall and around the corner to Mr. Kraft's office. One that would make the door stick closed as soon as Mr. Pruitt went inside! The spell ought to last about half an hour. With luck, long enough for Sabrina to fix her latest mess!

Now Sabrina turned back to that little brat, Libby.

"Nanny, nanny, boo-boo! You can't catch me!"

Sabrina couldn't help herself.

Zaaaaap! Libby's feet stuck to the floor like glue.

"Help!" Libby cried, struggling to move her feet. "I'm stuck!"

Sabrina ran up to her and held out her hand. "Give me my necklace back, and I'll help you."

Libby pouted. But at last she handed over the locket.

Reluctantly Sabrina unglued Libby's feet.

Libby wiggled one foot. "I'm still gonna tell my mommy," she muttered.

One good thing about doing her magic around her classmates in this condition: Kids were used to Santa Claus, tooth fairies, and imaginary friends. A little bit of magic didn't freak them out.

"Okay, everybody!" Sabrina called, clapping her hands. "I need you all to come over here for a minute!"

The kids scattered in all directions, mostly ignoring her.

Sabrina groaned. *Kindergarten teachers are definitely underpaid,* she thought. How did they get a mob of children to sit down and pay attention?

She thought back to her own kindergarten teacher, Mrs. Touchstone. She was Sabrina's favorite teacher ever. What would she do?

"Children!" Sabrina called out. "If everyone's sitting here on their bottoms by the time I count to ten, I'll tell you a nice story. With candy and everything."

Her friends stampeded to center stage, squirming and jostling each other as they hurried to sit down.

"Very good," Sabrina said, smiling down at their innocent upturned faces. Most of them looked so cute! Especially Harvey. He must have been an adorable little boy.

Sabrina held up the shiny golden locket and slowly began to swing it.

"Is this a story about a locket?" asked Libby, wiping her running nose with the back of her hand.

As Libby would say—ew! Sabrina dug a tissue out of her pocket and handed it to the cheerleader. "Yes, Libby," she said. "Sort of. Now, just look closely at the locket . . ."

Slowly, one by one, their eyes drifted closed.

> *"Remember your ages*
> *and all the stages.*
> *Then to now, go year by year.*
> *Remember it all, until you're here.*
> *First grade, second grade. . . ."*

Using the same kind of hypnotic magic that she'd used to get her friends into kindergarten, Sabrina took her friends forward into first grade, second grade . . . fifth grade . . .

"Boys are so gross!" Valerie mumbled.

Sixth grade . . .

"Arnold Tysinger is so cute!" Valerie moaned.

Seventh grade . . .

"Eek! A zit!" Libby shrieked. "My life is over!"

Eighth grade, ninth grade . . .

And so on until at last they were in the present. Now, to get them back to exactly the right moment.

That should be it! Slowly she counted backward to awaken them from their trance.

Immediately half the girls began crying on one another's shoulders. Valerie covered her face with her Tiny Tim cap. Harvey was moaning, holding his head in his hands. Libby was shouting, blaming everybody in sight.

"This is going to be the worst night of my life!" Libby squealed, jumping to her feet. "My Oscar chances are going to be, like, totally blown forever!"

Oops! Sabrina thought. *Looks like I took them just a little too far.*

She quickly got everyone settled down again and back into their memories.

It was kind of like trying to park a car in a tight spot using a stick shift. A little forward, a little backward.

At last she thought she had them at the right spot.

"Harvey," she asked gently, while they still had their eyes closed. "Do you remember your line?"

"Sure," Harvey said. He cleared his throat and raised an imaginary glass in a toast. "To Mr. Scrooge!"

"Mr. Scrooge!" Libby sneered. "That stingy old man?"

"Woo-hoo!" Sabrina cheered. "Bull's-eye!"

She made a few more spot checks. Yes! It appeared that all the cast members remembered their lines.

Now, she quickly wiped the last memories from their minds up to the present. It was kind of like erasing a tiny section on a videotape. Just the part that covered Sabrina walking under the ladder, ruining everything, and using Insta-Magic.

Then she brought everyone out of the trance.

"Hey, guys," she said brightly, glancing at her

watch. "We're running out of time. We'd better get going."

The cast members hurried to take their marks.

"Harvey, I think we stopped with you," the stage manager said. "Your line is—"

"Don't tell me," Harvey said, holding up his hand. "I remember." As Bob Cratchit sat at his humble table with his large happy family, he raised his glass in a toast and said, "To Mr. Scrooge!"

"Mr. Scrooge?" Libby, as Mrs. Cratchit, snapped. "That stingy old man?"

"Well," said Harvey. "It is Christmas . . ."

"All right, then," said Libby. So they toasted Mr. Scrooge—but not very loudly.

"And God bless us every one," Valerie, as Tiny Tim, chirped happily.

As they broke for a scene change, they heard clapping from the audience.

"Terrific!" Mr. Pruitt called.

Whoops! Forgot about him! How long was he watching?

"Where have you been, Mr. Pruitt?" Libby asked. "You missed my best scene."

Mr. Pruitt looked flustered. "I, uh—got stuck in Mr. Kraft's office . . ."

Sabrina couldn't help herself. She began to giggle.

"What's so funny!" Libby demanded. She looked herself over, checking for something wrong with her costume.

"Nothing!" Sabrina gasped, catching her breath. "Everything's absolutely perfect."

Libby opened her mouth —and froze.

So did Harvey, Valerie, Lloyd, and all the rest of the crew and cast. Even Mr. Pruitt.

Now what? Sabrina thought frantically. Some residual side effect from her afternoon's patch-work magic?

And then she felt someone appear behind her.

She didn't have to look. She knew who it was.

"I wouldn't say *absolutely* perfect, exactly," the Quizmaster said.

She turned around. As usual he was dressed outrageously—this time in the opulent fur-trimmed robes of the Ghost of Christmas Present.

"Cute," Sabrina said sarcastically.

"Thanks." He adjusted his crown of holly leaves.

"So, why do I have a feeling you had something to do with all this?" Sabrina asked.

"Because you're psychic?" the Quizmaster quipped. Then he cleared his throat and said, in an absolutely perfect imitation of Sabrina's voice: *"Insta-Magic . . . Wipe their minds . . ."*

And boy, did it look weird coming out of his mouth!

Sabrina sputtered, *"You?* You're my inner voice?"

The Quizmaster shrugged. "Hey, whatever you want to call it."

Sabrina buried her face in her hands. "I can't believe it! I can't believe I let you fake me out like that!"

"It does seem a little unbelievable," the Quizmaster agreed. He looked at the calendar on his wristwatch. "After all, it's already Friday. I might have thought you'd gotten a little more hip to my temptations by now."

"Argghhhh!"

"I had a feeling you might say that."

Sabrina nudged the frozen Tiny Tim aside and sat down on the edge of the chair at the Cratchits' table. "So," she said in resignation. "I guess I failed this latest test—big time."

"Well, yes, you did fail to resist the temptation to clean up your act with Insta-Magic and by erasing everyone's memory."

Too bad I'm not really the Ghost of Christmas Past, she thought. *Then maybe I could go back into my past—before I broke that magic mirror and brought on all this bad luck!*

"However," the Quizmaster added, "I will put a notation in your record that you used one of the great classics of literature to clean up your mess."

"Woo-hoo," Sabrina said sarcastically. She propped her elbows on the table, with her chin in her hands, and looked around at her friends, frozen in time.

"Oh, well," she said with a half smile. "I guess at least *this time* it was worth it."

The Quizmaster looked at her quizzically. "Say what? How so, little one?"

"My bad luck didn't just hurt me this time," Sabrina explained. "It caused me to nearly ruin the play that my friends worked so hard on. I guess I couldn't let that be, even if it did mean I had to flunk your stupid—"

The Quizmaster glared.

"I mean, your highly educational test."

"Much better."

"So it cost me. But I'm glad I was at least able save the play." She smiled, really smiled for the first time since she walked under that ladder. "I'll just consider it an early Christmas present to my friends."

The Quizmaster did something then that surprised Sabrina.

He *didn't* answer with a snappy comeback. In fact, he just stood there, deep in thought.

And then he smiled at her and held out his hand. A tiny gold-wrapped box appeared in his palm.

"What's that?" Sabrina asked.

"A present. For you." He held it out to her. "Go ahead. Open it."

She reached for the present, then jerked her hand back, as if afraid something in the package might bite. "Wait a minute. This is a trick—another temptation, right?"

The Quizmaster shook his head. "Hey, one temptation quiz a day is my limit. Promise. Now go ahead. Open it."

And so she did.

Inside was a small coupon. It said: 50 PERCENT OFF.

"Fifty percent off?" Sabrina asked, confused. "Off what?"

The Quizmaster grinned. "Your flunking grade. I'm going to give you half credit on this one."

"But why?" she exclaimed. Then, "I mean, great, fine—I accept!" She grinned, then peered at him. "But how come?"

"Well, you did fail the test and give in to temptation, but it was for a good cause. To help others. And I think that counts for something."

"You can do that?" she asked.

"Hey, I'm your Quizmaster! Yes, I can do it!"

"Woo-hoo!" she shouted, for real this time.

Sabrina couldn't help herself; she gave him a quick hug.

"Hey, don't be thinking you can butter me up, now."

"I'm not," she said. "But hey, I didn't get you anything!"

"Yeah, you did," he said.

"What?"

"A warm, fuzzy feeling," the Quizmaster replied. "And I tell you, I don't get those very often. At least, not when there's no chocolate involved."

Sabrina laughed.

"Well, to borrow one of your phrases, Sabrina—gotta go!" He snapped his fingers and disappeared. "See you around . . ."

Sabrina's smile faded just a notch. *That's what I'm afraid of!* she thought. She still had one more day of bad luck to go.

Oh, well. At least she'd seen the last of him for today. And now—the play must go on!

She turned to her friends. They were still frozen, in what looked like a card from *A Christmas Carol*. "Hey, Fizzmaster!" she hollered. "You forgot to—"

"Sorry!" he hollered back.

And then the cast and crew were all scrambling to finish the rehearsal.

Sabrina sighed in relief. Then she hurried backstage to see if she could help with any last-minute details—very careful to completely avoid the ladder on her way.

And just before she went onstage that night, she heard her "inner voice" whisper in her ear the traditional good-luck wish of the theater: *"Break a leg . . ."*

"Quizmaster!" she shrieked, looking around.

Then she spotted him through the curtain—grinning from ear to ear as he sat in the front row with her aunts, waiting for the play to begin.

Ooooh! Sabrina thought, shaking her fist at him. *Just wait till I see you tomorrow!*

Another corner piece of the mirror floated smoothly into the rest.

"Yes! One more piece and I can go back to reflecting instead of foreshadowing!"

SATURDAY

Reflections in a Mirror Crack'd Up

*By David Cody Weiss and
Bobbi JG Weiss*

Sabrina sat on the couch in the living room amid a mountain of pillows, an enormous bowl of popcorn on the wicker chest in front of her, glazed eyes fixed on the flickering TV screen. Hilda breezed down the stairs on her way to the kitchen, walked past, did a double take, and returned to the living room.

"What are *you* doing home on a Saturday night?" she asked.

Sabrina looked guiltily at her aunt. "I'm grounded, remember?"

"Oops!" Hilda said. She made a wry face. "Did you have a date?"

Sabrina sunk back behind her pillows. "Yes, Harvey asked me out. So did Dashiell, for that matter. I told them both no."

Hilda was stunned. "Let me get this straight. You were asked out by both your hot new hunk

197

and your steady, and you told them both no? You didn't ask either one to come over *here?* Have I taught you nothing? How can you be so wasteful? There are people dateless in many countries. There are people dateless in this house, for that matter."

"I'm sorry for you, Aunt Hilda, but you know what this week has been like. There's one more day of bad luck left to that mirror curse. Nothing happened so far today. If I have company over now, I'll run straight into it." Sabrina hugged a pillow protectively. "I'm staying right here by myself where it's safe until tomorrow."

"Running away from a curse never helps, you know. I once stole a guy away from another witch and she put a curse on me so that I would be hideously embarrassed in public. I tried hiding in a bunker for twenty-five years to avoid it. When I finally gave up, I found that they'd built a YMCA over the crypt, and I came up in the middle of the locker room. I was mortified—I hadn't done my hair in a year!" Hilda gestured at the TV set. "What *is* that you're watching, anyway?"

"It's a new cable channel they just launched called Trash TV. They're kicking it off with a *Gary Slummer Show* marathon. So far I've watched 'My Mother, My Self—Clones Speak Out,' 'I'm My Own Best Friend—People Who Answered Their Own Personal Ads,' and 'Kids Who Were Rejected by Their Imaginary Friends.'

Now they're doing 'What Was I Thinking?—Secrets I Should Never Have Revealed.'"

"I heard that the Slummer show was going to be canceled because they'd had an episode where there *wasn't* a fight."

"It almost was, but then they got into a fight with the people who wanted to cancel them and they filmed that to make up for it. They showed that episode first."

"Well, I'm sorry to interrupt the *Saturday Night Fights,* but I usually watch the *Amazing, Incredibly Real, Celebrity Psychic Hotline* at this time." With that, Hilda sat down on the couch.

"And you think I'm watching trash," Sabrina chided her. "I never knew you watched that show."

"That's because you have dates on Saturday nights and I don't," Hilda said sourly. Then she brightened and waggled her index finger. "Anyway, I like to use my magic to make the psychics *really* able to tell the callers' futures. It freaks them out big time."

Sabrina giggled, then immediately sobered up again when Hilda confiscated the TV remote control and changed the channel. *Amazing, Incredibly Real, Celebrity Psychic Hotline* was just starting. "C'mon, Aunt Hilda, I can't leave. I'll get into trouble again."

Hilda's eyes were already glued to the program. "A curse is a curse, Sabrina," she said with irritating cheerfulness. "There's no running away from it. You can't avoid your own future, especially when magic's involved. Besides, you don't have to leave the house—you can watch your shows on the portable TV."

"We don't have a portable TV."

Hilda flicked her finger at the ceiling. "Check your desk," she said with a smirk.

Sabrina levitated her pillows and popcorn, towing them behind her as she trudged upstairs to her bedroom. As she entered the room, she heard Salem laughing. He was perched on the chair in front of her desk, cackling at a large portable TV.

He shot Sabrina a guilty look as she came in. "I didn't steal it," he said defensively. "It just appeared here. Honest."

"For once I believe you, since I already know where it came from," Sabrina said, motioning her pillows down onto the bed and the popcorn onto the desk. She flicked a finger to change the channel.

"Hey, I was watching that!" objected Salem. "I love it when those psychics suddenly start telling the truth. Their eyes bug out and they look like they're going to drop their teeth."

The *Gary Slummer Show* came back on, but now Sabrina couldn't concentrate on other people who felt their lives were in ruins. Her mind kept wandering back to the mirror she'd broken at the beginning of the week. It seemed like an eternity ago, yet here she was, still suffering for it by spending a Saturday night at home. After the craziness of this week and last night's play, she really wanted to cut loose. She sprawled over her pillows and pouted. "Salem, did you ever do something that you felt ruined your life?"

"Duh—I'm a cat, aren't I?" Salem snorted. "Actually, I don't regret trying to take over the world. I do, however, regret getting caught."

"I wish there was some way to see what the future holds so I could avoid doing things I'd regret later."

Salem turned to face her, his golden eyes alight. "Throw together a Peek-Ahead potion."

"Huh? I've never seen one of those in my spellbook."

"Well, it's sort of an ad-lib," Salem admitted. "You mix together a Personal Essence extract and a Probability spell."

"Wait a minute." The memory of glass shards flitted through Sabrina's memory, all those little bits of bad luck just waiting to get her. "Didn't the Quizmaster say that mixing spells could lead to big trouble?"

"They only say that so you buy Witch Union products. All the warnings are the same—perform only under the supervision of an adult 500 or older; don't try this at home, kids, we're trained professionals; your mileage may vary— it's all legalistic yadda yadda to keep innovation to a limit. Like, the same people who eat sweet-and-sour sauce think ketchup and honey sandwiches are gross."

Sabrina made a face. "Yuck! Maybe because it *is* gross!"

"Hey," Salem pressed, "if nobody had thought to combine chocolate and peanuts, those kids would never have made friends with ET in that movie."

"I guess," Sabrina said. "Life *would* be a lot easier if you knew what was going to happen to you." She lugged her big spellbook from its stand onto the desk and thumbed through it until she found the directions for making a Personal Essence extract. "It says that I need to mix together the unique elements of my life, apply pressure, then drain off the vital juices. Care to translate that?"

Salem put his front paws on the book and peered down at the print. "The Table of Unique Elements says that you need to place items that represent the best and worst of your life into an enclosed container that best characterizes your essential existence. In my case, that would mean I'd put my first edition copy of *Benevolent Despots of History* and a bottle of deworming medicine into a litter box. For you—"

"It would have to be stuff from my life as a half-witch and a half-mortal." Sabrina's eyes scanned the room, then lit up. "The cauldron Aunt Hilda and Aunt Zelda gave me on the day I discovered that I was a witch combines both. Perfect! I can put the ingredients in there."

She emptied out the collection of pens and

pencils that normally filled the small iron cauldron and moved it to the center of her desk.

"Start with three equal parts of your current environment," Salem read from the recipe.

Sabrina began examining things in her room, trying to decide what best represented her life. A thought suddenly struck her. "I need to choose stuff that's significant to me, right? But anything like that will be something I don't want to destroy. How do we get around that?"

"Easy," replied Salem. "We're only going for essence here. Nothing will get damaged. Just shrink the ingredients small enough to fit into the cauldron, and when we're done, you can return them to their original size."

"Okay, then." Sabrina moved to her book shelf. "I can use my Westbridge High yearbook, since that's where I spend most of my time and it has nearly everybody I know in it."

"Remember to balance the positives and negatives."

"The positives would be a Valentine's Day card from Harvey, the shoes we danced the night away in, and my sash with all of my Scout merit badges." As she spoke, Sabrina plucked up each item.

"I wanted to be a Scout as a kid," Salem reminisced, "until I found out that you don't become a Scoutmaster by staging a coup."

Sabrina ignored him and continued grabbing up items. "And the negatives would be the picture of our school play cast with Libby, a letter from Kraft demanding a parent-teacher conference, and the school lunch menu." A flick of her finger shrank all the objects to dollhouse size. She dropped them into the cauldron.

Salem got a glance at the school lunch menu before it shrank. "Do they really get federal money to feed you *that?*" he asked.

"Hey—you eat stinky fish and meat by-products, whatever they are."

"So feed me caviar and filet mignon, I won't complain."

"Our household budget would." Sabrina tilted her head at the cat. "What's next?"

Salem looked down at the page. "Something to represent your hopes and dreams."

"Hmm, that's a tough one. There are so many things I'd like to do. I don't want to exclude anything. What do you think?"

"I'm a cat, not a guidance counselor. Besides, I wanted *everything,* remember?"

As if she were shopping in her own bedroom, Sabrina wandered about, zapping up things as she thoughtfully evaluated them. "Let's see. How about a happy home life . . ." She floated in some of her aunts' magazines from the hall table, starting with *House & Gargoyle Magazine* and *Perpetual Bride.* "Career . . ." In went *Nobel Prize Review* and *Scientific Thaumaturgy.* "And something for good citizenship." A copy of the Constitution and a Save the Whales poster flew into the cauldron.

"Now for the Peek-Ahead potion ingredients," said Salem, and as he read, Sabrina zapped up the items, shrunk them down, and popped them in with the other ingredients. "Start with a perpetual calendar to represent time, then add some prune juice as a symbol of old age. And for the seeing-into-the-future part, you have a choice—a telescope for the far future, binoculars for middle future, or opera glasses for the middle of next week."

"I'll go with the binoculars," Sabrina decided.

"Now add pressure."

"What symbolizes pressure?"

"Well, think about having to decide how to spend a life that will last a thousand years—*right now!*" ordered Salem.

Caught off guard like that, Sabrina felt beads of sweat immediately pop up on her brow.

"There you go," said Salem triumphantly.

Sabrina wiped her brow and flung the drops into the cauldron. The black iron pot trembled and spouted a column of steam. It began to tip first one way, then the other as its trembling grew stronger and stronger.

"Now pour the essence onto a crystal ball," instructed Salem.

Hesitantly Sabrina reached out to the cauldron, which was dancing back and forth now, spouting steam and rattling everything on her desk top. She gingerly picked it up, then exclaimed, "Rats! Aunt Zelda took the crystal ball to her Saturday night symposium. She's expecting a callback from the Nobel Prize committee."

"She's dreaming," snorted Salem. "If they knew she was a witch, they'd never even consider her work. Pure academic jealousy, if you ask me."

Sabrina eyed the portable TV. "What about that?"

"I don't know, magic and electronics don't always work well together. That's why there's no reliable computerized spell-checkers." Salem considered the set. "Is it cable-ready?"

"I think so."

"If you're willing to risk it," he replied. "Be sure to unplug it first."

Sabrina unplugged the set and then carefully tilted the cauldron over the TV. A thin stream of rainbow twinkles slid over the iron lip and down into the set. She put the cauldron back down then, and, scooching her chair closer to the desk, sat down and stared into the screen.

The blank surface of the set silvered and settled into a mirror-like reflection of Sabrina's own face. It reminded her uncomfortably of the broken mirror that had started this troublesome week. *At least things can't go wrong while I'm sitting here safe at home,* she thought.

Then the room burst into riotous swirls of light, spiraling like a whirlpool into a dark center spot on the screen. The whirlpool spun faster and faster around her until it made Sabrina dizzy. There was a moment of weightlessness, then, with a yelp of surprise, she disappeared, literally sucked into the TV screen.

"Hmmm," said Salem. *"That* wasn't supposed to happen."

The phone rang constantly, its multiple lines receiving new calls as fast as the old ones hung up. The black cat spoke at ninety miles an hour into a specially made headset that attached to his collar. "Witchway Foundation, Salem speaking, please hold. Witchway Foundation, Salem speaking, please hold. Witchway Foundation, Salem speaking, please hold. Witchway Foundation, Salem speaking, please—oh, you're already holding? Well, hold some more."

He pressed a button on the phone with a paw. "Hi, still there? Okay, as I was saying, you submit your request . . . sorry, only one per applicant . . . and it's entered into our database. Applications are chosen at random by an independent accounting firm . . . yes, just like the award shows use . . . and then are rated for difficulty, probability, cost-effectiveness, and environmental impact. Price quotes are sent back to the applicant, and if the terms are agreed on, then the project is added to the job queue. Payment is required in advance, and all profits above operating costs are donated to charity by a rotating lottery system. We don't do sports scores, TV ratings, personal harm, product endorsements, or election-fixing. Sorry, nobody—not even a witch—does windows." Salem's head snapped backward at the caller's comment. "Oh, yeah? Well, that goes double back atcha, bub! And remember, we *can* make it happen!"

The cat batted the speakerphone angrily, breaking the connection. He batted a second button to switch the answering machine on and trotted into the kitchen. A haggard-looking Sabrina was there making the day's seventh pot of coffee.

"We're running late, kid," Salem told her. "Here's the afternoon's agenda. We have seven lost pets to locate, two instant house remodelings, two and a quarter tons of flab to banish for the weight-loss clients, and the Board of Sahara called to say that they need less rain this month because mildew is starting to grow on everything.

"On the bad news side, kids still won't eat their broccoli, even the chocolate-flavored kind, and the 'Get-a-Geek-a-Life' program is a complete bust. Apparently there are things even magic can't change."

Sabrina slumped into a chair at the table, too tired to lift the cup of cold coffee that sat there. "I don't know how much more of this I can handle," she moaned.

"Shoulda thought of that before you outed yourself and set up business as America's only public witch."

"It seemed like a good idea at the time."

"And I'm sure that buying tickets for the *Titanic* did, too."

Sabrina leaned forward and tiredly cradled her head in her arms. "I wanted to live an honest life, not hiding all the time. And I wanted to do some good in the world."

"So did I," countered Salem, "but the world didn't have the good grace to surrender to me."

"I do miss my family, though."

"Your aunts have better sense than to live in the center of a hurricane."

Sabrina managed a weak chuckle. "I've been dreaming of living in the center of a hurricane. I hear that it's quiet there." The private videophone line chimed. "Case in point." She limply signaled acceptance of the call. Libby Chessler's face appeared, a hologram hanging in midair.

"Afternoon, Mayor," Sabrina sighed. "What is it now?"

"Sabrina," cooed Westbridge's four-term leader, "we've been friends for a long time now—"

"Isn't that what Brutus said to Julius Caesar?" snorted Salem.

"Long enough for me to even grow to appreciate your pet's irreverent sense of humor." Libby's face slipped into a practiced frown of parental-style disapproval. "That's why I feel so . . . disappointed that you chose not to help your community more."

"Excuse me?" Sabrina said wearily. "What

about the twenty hours of community service I perform? All those self-delivering meals for poor people?"

"Well, that's all well and good for poor people. They're probably satisfied with SlummerNet and free food. But the better people in Westbridge, the *important* people, are concerned why you haven't done anything to attract business to our town or to help increase property values."

"My job is—and since I'm the one who wrote my own job description, I know it intimately—to use my powers to help ordinary people cope with the hardships of life."

Libby's composure slipped and she snapped bitterly, "What about the hardships of *political* life? My backers expected a return for their endorsement. Your . . . *nonperformance* has cost me and my party the governorship."

"I'm apolitical, remember? Who wins and who loses makes no difference to me."

"Oh, but it does now," said Libby. "My party is unhappy. Unhappy enough to wonder whether someone so unusual, so powerful, can be trusted if they misuse those powers."

"Me, misuse my powers?" Sabrina shouted, suddenly energized by a wave of anger. "All I *do* is help people! It's *all* I seem to do nowadays."

"Really. Magical makeovers? Rounding up stray animals? Greening places the citizens of Westbridge will never see? Useless, all of it."

Libby's eyes narrowed to little slits. "What about fires, floods, auto accidents?"

"I try to help whenever something happens—"

"But why should they happen at all, my party wonders. Why aren't you *preventing* them?"

So that was it. As usual, Libby was looking for special favors, ones that even Sabrina couldn't give. "Nobody can predict the future," Sabrina stated, "not even witches. Any peek forward is a guess. There's no way of telling what's actually going to happen."

Mayor Libby adopted her best "compassionate" look. "That's a tragically misguided position to take. My party disagrees. In fact, my party thinks that you should be held *liable* for damages that occur from disasters you don't *prevent."*

Sabrina leaped to her feet. *"What?* That's the stupidest thing I've ever heard! You tell your party leader he's insane!"

The videophone's holographic receiver swelled until it nearly filled the kitchen. For the first time, Sabrina could see that Mayor Libby was calling from a courtroom—a courtroom in full session and televised by a platoon of cameras. A familiar face presided from the high bench.

Libby smiled nastily. "Oh, you shouldn't have said that, Sabrina. He's a judge, and insulting him is contempt of court." She nodded to the black-robed figure. "Isn't that right, Judge Slummer?"

Libby's face grew to fill the giant holo-screen.

"You're going to do things our way or you're going to go down—way down, Sabrina. Nobody will help you because, in spite of all your good works, you're too *different."* The first honest emotion lit up the mayor's face. Contempt. "Once a freak, always a freak."

Her face exploded into millions of colorful shards, swirling in spirals and knots . . .

Sabrina felt herself sucked inside out and tossed through the air. She found herself sitting in front of her desk in her bedroom, the portable TV's screen a sheet of fading rainbow sparkles. A moment later, the screen reverted to gray glass, reflecting her face and its confused expression.

"Whu' happen'?" she asked, shaking her head and feeling quite woozy.

"I think you had some bad spell interaction. You got sucked into the TV instead of just viewing it. It was interesting to watch, though."

"Well, it wasn't interesting to *live* through!"

"Could have had something to do with your channel selection," Salem mused. "The TV was still set to the Gary Slummer marathon. Maybe you'd have better results tuning in to PBS."

"Salem," Sabrina said fearfully, "is that what my future is really going to be like?"

"Beats me. But if it is, you'll be the only person whose future will be multiple choice."

Sabrina sat and thought a moment. Then she shook her head. "No, Salem, I think everybody's future is multiple choice—until you choose one. And even then, you still can't control what happens. I tried to avoid the broken-mirror curse by hiding at home and it found me, even here." She smiled. "On the other hand, that means my future is curse-free and I *can* go out if I want to." She grabbed up the phone. "I wonder if Harvey or Dashiell is still available for a date?"

Now the mirror had both eyes. "There we go. That's perfect! I can—"

She stopped. There was still a piece of the mirror missing. "My nose!"

Indeed, the center was missing and the other pieces were starting to drift around the surface without their anchor. "How did this *happen? This has* never *happened before! Seven days! That's the deal! Seven pieces, seven days. I can't imagine what this means."*

So the mirror looked ahead.

"Oh, dear," she muttered. "That poor girl. She will never *see this coming . . ."*

SUNDAY

Mom vs. Magic
*A novelization by David Cody Weiss
and Bobbi JG Weiss
Based upon the episode written
by Sheldon Bull*

Midnight.

Sabrina lay on her bed, heaving a sigh of relief. It was *over*. Her horrible, awful, embarrassing, nerve-wracking, annoying, and all-round lousy-rotten-stinky week of bad luck was finally over. In a fit of happiness she leaped to her feet and danced around her bedroom. "It's o-ver!" she sang, "it's a-a-all o-ver, yippee!"

Feeling free and easy for the first time in seven days, she flung open her bedroom door and, still dancing, boogied down the hall. "O-ver, it's o-ver, an' I'm still here, ooooh yeah, baby!"

Actually, Sabrina's bad luck was over, but she knew full well that her life of weirdness certainly wasn't. A teenage witch in a mortal world could not lead an "ordinary" life, period. But she was doing a pretty good job, smashed mirrors or no smashed mirrors.

As Sabrina be-bopped down the stairs, she heard Salem's voice from the kitchen. He was using the phone again, even though he really wasn't supposed to. After all, cats can't have credit cards, so whenever Salem got the urge to order a jumbo catnip mousie or a box of puppy-shaped snacks from his Kitty Kingdom mail order catalogue, he used Zelda's credit card. It simply never occurred to him that Zelda might not like that.

But then Sabrina realized that the cat wasn't making a mail order call. In fact, he sounded depressed. "Okay," he said in a hollow tone. "Fine. See ya." Click. Then, "No! Nooooo . . ."

Sabrina entered the kitchen to find Salem on the counter, sobbing next to the cordless phone. "What's the matter?" she asked him. "Ringworm got you down?"

"My mother is coming for a visit," Salem blubbered dismally. "I called to wish her a happy holiday and—oh, why didn't I just send the dry roasted almonds like I usually do?"

Holiday? Sabrina felt her good mood slip away, like a glacier cracking off the side of a cliff to vanish into the sea. She'd been so wrapped up in her bad-luck week she'd totally forgotten! Then again, what did mortal holidays matter to her? She couldn't see her mother anyway, no matter how much she wanted to. She couldn't even telephone her.

So much for her bad luck being over. Maybe

it was only beginning. Sabrina plopped down into a chair, as if the weight of her own body was suddenly too much to bear. "Salem, you should be happy she's coming. I haven't seen my mother in over a year because I'm a witch, and she's a mortal, and if I even look at her she'll turn into a ball of wax, which is the stupidest rule in the—"

"Hey! We were talking about me!"

Something odd in Salem's tone of voice made Sabrina suspicious. Eyeing his fuzzy black face, she asked, "Your mom knows you're now a cat, right?"

At that, Salem burst into tears again.

"Salem, how could you keep this a secret?"

"It slipped my mind?" Salem sighed. "You don't understand. My mother is very critical. I once wore sandals to the dinner table and she sent me to military school."

"Were they flip flops? Because then I'm with her—"

"Sabrina, please, don't make me face my mother as a cat. She'll hate me!" He made his eyes go wide, trying for his best manipulative Bambi look. "Use your magic. Send me somewhere. Anywhere. I'm begging you!"

"Okay," Sabrina said, and pointed at him. Salem rose up from the counter, floated about five inches to one side, then floated back down again.

He frowned. "Thanks. She'll never see me here."

In the morning, Salem still hadn't managed to leave the Spellman household, though not for lack of trying. What good was it to live with three witches if they wouldn't do a simple favor now and then?

"Oh, no. There's Salem." Hilda spotted the cat on the wicker basket in front of the linen closet, his eyes closed.

Zelda continued forward on tip-toe. "Maybe he won't see us."

He saw them. "Pleeease . . ." he whined.

"We are not sending you to Palm Beach," said Zelda flatly.

"Okay, Tucson—Chattanooga—Moosejaw— anywhere!"

"She's your mother," Hilda reminded him. "She'll find you."

Zelda turned to her sister. "And I still think we should visit *our* mother."

At that Hilda squirmed. "I just don't feel like taking a long trip now."

"The trip to the Other Realm takes a fiftieth of a second."

"You know how easily I get bored."

Zelda gave up and reached out to open the linen closet just as thunder clapped and a bright light flashed from under the door. When the door swung open, Sabrina stepped out with Dashiell, a cute half-witch boy she'd been dating recently. They were holding hands.

"Aunt Zelda! Aunt Hilda!" Sabrina blushed and immediately dropped Dashiell's hand. "I didn't expect to find you standing . . . right here."

"That's one of the problems with having your linen closet as a portal to the Other Realm," Zelda said dryly. "Every now and then, you need towels."

Hilda gave a cheerful little wave. "Hi, Dashiell. How was the brunch? Where'd you go? What'd you do? Anyone get kissed?"

Quickly Zelda grabbed a stack of towels and piled them into Hilda's arms, covering her sister's face. "We'll leave you two alone," she told Sabrina, and scooping up Salem in one arm, she pulled Hilda away with the other.

Sabrina watched them go. "We're her legal guardians," Hilda was whispering to Zelda. "We're morally obligated to snoop!"

Dashiell was amused. "I hope you had fun this morning," he said.

Sabrina marveled at Dashiell's choice of dating activity. "I loved it. Sliding all the way from Canada to Mexico on that glacier was amazing." She rubbed a sore spot. "Except for the whole raw butt thing."

Dashiell chuckled. "You're the most wonderful, amazing girl I've ever been out with." He leaned forward just a little.

Sabrina found herself leaning forward a little,

too. "You must be a mind reader," she said, "because that's exactly what I wanted to hear."

Their lips were just about to touch when Sabrina spotted Hilda peeking around a corner. Pointing her finger, the teenage witch zapped a door into the hallway to block her aunt's view.

"Now I know how Mormons feel," Hilda grumbled from behind the new obstruction. But any other grumbling she might have added was lost to Sabrina, who didn't hear or see anything but fireworks as Dashiell kissed her.

They parted slowly. "I've always heard that, if you enjoyed a kiss, then the other person probably enjoyed it, too," Dashiell ventured hopefully.

"Really? I've never heard that." Sabrina felt her cheeks flush with pleasure. "Yes, I did," she assured him.

Reluctantly, Dashiell stepped back into the linen closet. "'Bye," he said simply, and with a clap of thunder and a flash of lightning, he was gone.

The next day at school, Sabrina opened her locker to find a beautiful rose floating inside. "Oh, Dash . . . ."

"Hey."

At the sound of Harvey's voice, Sabrina grabbed the rose. Having a symbol of love in her locker was going to be hard enough to explain, let alone the fact that it could float. However, she forgot about the thorns. "Oww!"

Harvey sauntered up and peeked into her locker. "Where'd you get the rose?"

"Found it," Sabrina blurted, sucking her injured thumb. "So, what's new in your life?"

"Actually, I need a favor. Could you help me buy a present for my mom? Last time I got her a can opener. I *have* to stop taking gift advice from my dad." He paused. "You okay?"

Thoughts of her own mother were flooding Sabrina's mind. She realized she was frowning, so she forced a wistful smile and shrugged. "I miss my mom. She's still on that archaeology expedition in Peru."

"You should visit her."

"I would but I'm, uh . . . waiting for the ancient city of Machu Picchu to get an Arby's." Harvey just looked at her, confused. "So how does your mom feel about wine and cheese?" Sabrina asked, changing the subject.

"She finds it binding."

"Well, there's always jewelry . . . or bran." Nope, Harvey didn't get the joke. He looked so cute when he didn't understand her jokes—like a bewildered puppy. Sabrina gave his hand a squeeze. "We'll find something."

He grinned. "You're the best." And then, to her surprise, he leaned over and kissed her on the cheek. He'd already sauntered halfway down the hall by the time the fireworks in her head stopped and she could register reality again. Touching the spot where he kissed her, she murmured, "Oh, Harvey . . ."

Tap tap!

Sabrina spun around to find Dashiell's rose hovering over her shoulder. She snatched it out of midair before anybody saw it. "I've got a big problem."

"Hilda!"

"Coming!"

Zelda headed for the linen closet, pulling a suitcase on wheels behind her. Hilda hurried to catch up, carrying a little overnight bag. "Why are you so resistant to the idea of seeing our own mother?" Zelda asked her sister.

"Because she likes you better than she likes me," Hilda grumped.

"What? That's ridiculous. She loves us both exactly the same." Zelda paused. "Perhaps she *should* like me more, but I don't think she does."

"How come on your eighth birthday you got an entire observatory and I got corrective shoes?"

"I like stars and you had those funny toes." Zelda stopped at the wicker basket, staring down at it with suspicion. "Is Salem back in the hamper again?"

"No," answered Salem's voice.

Zelda hauled him out of the hamper. "Hello, Braveheart."

He cringed. "Don't make me face her!"

"See?" said Hilda. "No one wants to be with their mother. That's why they have a billion dollar greeting card industry."

Zelda set the cringing cat on the closed hamper lid. Salem hunkered down, looking like a kitten in the rain. "We're leaving, Salem. Tell Sabrina to zap in something healthy for dinner, not just Fluffernutter. And don't try to escape through your cat door because I nailed it shut." She opened the linen closet, and Hilda followed her inside.

"Mother never loved me when I was human," Salem called to them as the door closed. "One little hug, and I wouldn't have tried to take over Poland!" He got no answer but a crack of thunder and a flash of lightning. Burying his nose between his front paws, he began to sob.

The school bell rang, and suddenly the empty halls of Westbridge High swarmed with students. Sabrina hadn't yet joined the fray—she was still gathering up her books and belongings from the previous class. Just as she scooped everything up into her arms, Dashiell appeared. "What are you doing here?" she asked, both surprised and pleased to see him.

"I left my clone back at my school. I just hope I can read his notes this time." He gave her a wicked grin. "Want to become invisible and go give the queen a wedgie?"

Sabrina imagined giving Libby the ultimate wedgie and watching the cheerleader's eyes pop. "That sounds like fun." Then the image of Harvey giving his mother a can opener popped into her mind. "Oh, I can't. I promised Harv—a friend that I'd go shopping."

"Take a rain check." Dashiell pointed his finger at the nearest window, and an instant storm drenched everything outside. Three seconds later it was gone and the sun was shining again.

Touched by the magical display, Sabrina almost caved in. "I'd love to . . ." She caught herself. "But I can't break a promise."

They exited the classroom and stepped out into the hallway. Sabrina expected Dashiell to rag her for turning him down, but the half-witch boy actually looked impressed.

"Man, I like you," he said, and his eyes grew intense. Sabrina found herself drawn to them as if they were magnets. When Dashiell gazed at her, it was like he was gazing into her soul.

Then she saw Harvey out of the corner of her eye. He was talking to somebody, so he hadn't seen her yet. Thank goodness.

"Would you mind if I just stared at you all day?" Dashiell was murmuring dreamily, but he got no further as Sabrina pointed her finger at him. He vanished.

"I'll send you a picture," she apologized to the empty air.

Harvey sauntered up. Funny how he never

seemed to walk—he always sauntered. "Ready to go shopping?" he asked.

"Just let me get my chemistry book." Sabrina hurried to her locker and opened it up, only to find another rose, this one a different color, magically hovering inside. She snatched it up, careful of the thorns this time, but what could she possibly do with it? She wanted to keep it—Dashiell was such a sweetheart. But so was Harvey, and if he saw a *second* rose in her locker he'd certainly get suspicious. Then inspiration struck, and Sabrina whirled around, the rose outstretched in her hand. "For you."

Harvey took it, bewildered. "Gee . . . thanks." As they headed for the exit, he sniffed the rose, then glanced out the window with his confused puppy look. "Did it rain?"

The thunder and lightning that came from the Spellman linen closet was no storm. It was Salem's mother, Mrs. Saberhagen. She stepped out onto the carpet of the second-floor landing and peered curiously down the hallway, first one way, then the other. "Salem? Mother's here!"

"Momsie?"

It was Salem's voice, but he was nowhere to be seen. Baffled, the witch woman checked the hallway again. "Where are you?"

"Down here."

Only then did Mrs. Saberhagen notice the black feline sitting in the doorway of Sabrina's bedroom. Her eyebrows jumped high on her forehead. "Salem?"

The cat nodded unhappily.

"What on Earth happened?"

Resigned to his fate, Salem trotted over to the clothes hamper, leaped gracefully up onto the lid, and explained his dread secret at ninety miles an hour. "I tried to take over the world the Witches' Council sentenced me to a hundred years as a cat I eat off the floor and sleep by the dryer go ahead let me have it."

His mother frowned down at him. "Salem Saberhagen, you always disappoint me. You are selfish and irresponsible. You're a terrible person."

Salem cringed in shame.

"But if you aren't the cutest little kitty I've ever seen in my entire life!"

He blinked. "I am?"

Beaming with love, Mrs. Saberhagen held out her arms. "Come to mama!"

Amazed, Salem jumped into his mother's arms, and she gave him a hug that made his eyes bug. But he didn't mind. He was in ecstasy. His mother loved him! She was petting him! She was even scratching under his chin! He purred so loud he felt his ribs vibrate in rhythm, kind of like they did when he cranked up the volume on his Tony Orlando CDs. "Ummm . . . ahhh . . ." Then his mother's fashion fragrance hit his sensitive nostrils. "Chanel?" he wondered absently.

Later that afternoon, Dashiell appeared in the Spellman kitchen just as Sabrina and Harvey entered the front door of the house. "Sorry I couldn't make up my mind about a gift," Harvey was saying. "There was really nothing wrong with any of the sweaters you showed me, or the perfume—"

"Or the earrings," Sabrina added, "or the picture frames or the foot massagers . . ."

They walked to the living room and tiredly sank down on the couch. "I just really want this present for my mom to be perfect," Harvey continued earnestly.

"Especially since you wrecked the car last week."

He nodded. "And I kind of love her."

Sabrina smiled. That was the sort of statement that made her want to hug him. Little did she know that someone was in the kitchen at that moment, thinking about hugging *her*. Dashiell zapped a huge football-player-sized chocolate sundae into being, figuring that chocolate had to be her favorite flavor. Pleased with his magical handiwork, he bellowed out, "Sabrina!"

She heard the call and recognized his voice instantly.

"Who was that?" Harvey asked.

Sabrina's mind raced. "The oven," she blurted. "I forgot, I—I'm baking bread."

"An oven timer that calls you by name? Hey, maybe my mom would like one."

The call came again, this time from the dining room. "Sabrina?"

Sabrina leaped to her feet, grabbed Harvey's arm, and maneuvered him toward the front door. "Sorry, you have to go. I just remembered I have to set off a bug bomb. But we'll try shopping again tomorrow."

Harvey was definitely a stop-and-smell-the-roses kind of guy. Despite Sabrina's tugs, he ambled slowly after her, then simply stopped. "Can I ask you one more thing?"

It was times like this that Sabrina wished she were stronger. Maybe even a little intimidating. "Whatever it is, the answer is yes," she quipped, and tried to physically pull him to the door. He wouldn't budge. Instead, he beamed at her in delight.

"Really? So we can go steady again?"

Sabrina did a double take. *"Huh?"*

"Sabrina?" The doors leading to the dining room opened, and there stood Dashiell. Something that looked like a giant bowl of ice cream loomed behind him, but Sabrina didn't get a clear look at it. She was too busy watching Dashiell and Harvey discover each other's presence.

"Who's he?" they asked her in perfect unison.

There was no way out of this, so Sabrina tried for the casual approach. "Um . . . Harvey, Dashiell. Dashiell, Harvey."

The two young men didn't move. They didn't speak. They just looked at each other. Sabrina wanted to die.

"You won't believe this," she said, forcing cheerfulness, "but you guys have so much in common."

Moments later, all three of them were sitting in the living room with the chocolate sundae sitting before them like a calorie-infested mini-mountain. Totally flustered, Sabrina babbled as she handed each of them a spoon. "See, Harvey is a really close friend, or *was* until about five minutes ago when he asked me to go steady." She laughed nervously. Dashiell didn't join her. "And Dashiell is this new . . . person in my life, who I've sort of, very recently, been . . . seeing." She smiled at Harvey. For once, he didn't smile back. "Naturally, I was going to tell both of you about . . . both of you."

Silence.

Sabrina considered beating herself silly with the blunt end of her own spoon when Harvey finally spoke. "Well, we *said* we weren't going to be exclusive . . ." he admitted slowly.

"And we never talked about only seeing each other," Dashiell added thoughtfully.

Sabrina nearly fainted with relief. "Great! This is good. This is very good."

And then both young men locked eyes and said one word: "Choose."

Far, far away, Zelda Spellman was ringing the doorbell of her mother's house in the Other Realm. No one was answering. "That's odd," she said to Hilda beside her. "I told Mother we were coming."

"That's the problem. You told her *we* were coming. If it were just you, she'd be here, but since it's me, she's hiding under a pile of coats."

"You're being childish. I'll see if she left a key." Zelda lifted up the doormat to reveal an enormous skeleton key, at least two feet long. Triumphantly she picked it up.

Hilda only frowned. "More proof. She told me it was under the flower pot."

Zelda opened the door of their mother's house by touching the skeleton key to the door lock, and the two sisters entered.

Sabrina couldn't stand it any longer. Only a little while ago Dashiell and Harvey had ordered her to choose, but how could she? How could she decide which boy she liked best? She liked them both! A lot! Frustrated, she walked to the door.

"How about now?" Dashiell asked, tagging behind her.

"No," she answered.

"How about now?" Harvey asked, tagging behind Dashiell.

"No!" Sabrina swung the front door open. "I'll let you know when I decide. Just go."

Obediently, both boys left, casting her longing looks as they passed by. She closed the door with relief, but no sooner did she turn to leave when the doorbell rang. *"No!"* she yelled at it, and fled up the stairs where she found a woman she presumed to be Mrs. Saberhagen cradling Salem in her arms. Well, at least somebody was having a good time. "Hi, Mrs. Saberhagen."

"Hi," the witch woman answered, then she turned back to Salem and said in a cutesy baby-coo voice, "You're just a big ball of fluff, that's what you are. Isn't he just a big ball of fluff?"

In an ecstasy of pleasure, Salem slowly flexed his foreclaws in the air. "That's what he is, all right," he purred.

Annoyed, Sabrina hastened to the haven of her bedroom as Mrs. Saberhagen goo-gooed, "I'm going to make my boy a big fish dinner!"

"With *fish?"* Salem gasped in delight.

The sound of a soft *thud* reached Sabrina's ears—Salem jumping to the floor—and then Mrs. Saberhagen's footsteps descended the stairs. It really was nice that Salem enjoyed all the attention he was getting, but as far as Sabrina was concerned, she could do with a little less attention at the moment. "Both of you, go home!" she shouted out her window.

Down below on the sidewalk, Harvey and Dashiell hung their heads and trudged despondently away—in opposite directions.

Salem entered her room and jumped up on the bed. "Salem, can we talk?" she asked him, desperate for a sympathetic ear.

The cat just gazed into space, drunk with happiness. "Isn't my mother great? I mean, all mothers are great, but isn't my mother just plain better than anyone else's?"

"Harvey and Dashiell want me to choose between them," Sabrina said, "and I don't know what to do."

"Did I tell you she brushed me for hours this afternoon? It felt so silky good."

"You're not even listening to me!"

Salem's eyes came back into focus and he turned to her. "I am, too."

"Salem?" sang Mrs. Saberhagen's voice from downstairs, "you want to lick the deboning knife?"

Like a bolt of black lightning, Salem flashed out the door. "Gotta go! Good luck with the bake sale!"

What bake sale? He wasn't even listening! Fuming, Sabrina sat down at her desk. "Maybe I can't see my mother without turning her into a giant candle, but I don't see why I can't send her a letter." Taking pen and paper, she quickly wrote a note, then folded it into a paper airplane. "When it absolutely, positively has to be there in two seconds," she said in satisfaction, and launched the little plane into the air. As it soared, she pointed her index finger—the flying letter disappeared.

A blink of an eye later, Sabrina's "air mail" popped into existence on a mountaintop in the middle of Peru, right in front of her mother, who immediately recognized the magical item and snatched it up before her coworkers saw it.

Sabrina could only imagine what her mother was doing at the moment. Had she gotten the letter already? Was she reading it? Did she miss Sabrina as much as Sabrina missed her?

"Are you crazy?"

Startled, Sabrina whirled around to find her Quizmaster standing in the room, an angry expression on his face. Annoyed at the interruption, she shot back, "You wear those clothes and ask if *I'm* crazy?"

The Quizmaster ignored the insult. "Your mother is mortal!" he barked. "You are half witch! You are not allowed to send her letters until you get your witch's license, and that includes e-mail!"

Now Sabrina was angry. "You opened my paper airplane? Isn't that illegal?"

"I didn't read it. The Witches' Council did. And they are furious. They've handed down a decree." He snapped his fingers and, with a roar of thunder and a streak of magical lightning, a scroll appeared in his hand.

"Hey!" Sabrina's hands flew to her face. "I think you singed my eyebrows!"

The Quizmaster ignored her again. "Oh, boy," he murmured, reading, "this is worse than I ever imagined."

"What does it say?"

"Because you broke the rules, you have to choose between being a witch or seeing your mother." He looked up from the scroll and ominously finished, "Ever again."

It took a minute for Sabrina to speak. "It's unfair!" she finally exclaimed. "It's unjust! I bet it's even bad for the environment."

"It's the council." The Quizmaster shook his head, obviously thinking unpleasant thoughts. "They are one gaggle of bitter old witches."

Desperate, Sabrina threw her arms in the air. "No one ever said I couldn't write to my mother!"

"It's right here in the Magic Book," and the Quizmaster gestured at the big Magic Book that Sabrina's witch father had left her. It opened up and turned itself to a specific page.

Sabrina ripped that page out. "Not anymore!"

The Quizmaster could only shrug. Whether he agreed with the council or not didn't matter—an official decree was an official decree. He was just a messenger. "You have to choose between your mom or your magic," he reiterated. "You have twelve hours." And with that, he vanished.

Sabrina felt like tearing her hair out. "Wasn't choosing between boyfriends enough for one day?" she shouted.

The interior of the house reeked of Other Realmly quaintness. Zelda and Hilda looked around, poking through their mother's books and checking out the knickknacks. Hilda spotted a trophy and some parchments. "Winner of the Other Realm Science Fair, Zelda Spellman," she read on one. "Outstanding Student of the Decade, Zelda Spellman," she read on another. "Best of the Best, Zelda Spellman." She gave Zelda a narrow-eyed stare. "You're right. She loves us both the same."

"There must be something here of yours," Zelda said firmly, then spotted it. "Look. She kept your hat."

Hilda examined the old-fashioned hat and frowned. "She borrowed that two hundred years ago and never returned it."

"Really? She always returns everything she borrows from me."

Zelda realized too late that her comment hadn't helped. Hilda turned away from her, fuming.

Clouds of mist swirled and colors flared in and out, punctuated by the silvery sparkles of magic in motion. But no clear images formed. Sabrina gazed harder into her crystal ball. "Aunt Zelda? Aunt Hilda? Can you hear me? I need help!"

Finally someone answered—a recorded voice, crisp, polite, and completely irritating. *"The Other Realm customer you are trying to contact is either not available or has traveled outside our service area. Please try again later."* A phone somewhere in the magical ether hung up with a *click!*, and a dull dial tone issued from the crystal ball.

Sabrina yelled uselessly at it. "Hey, I'm supposed to have unlimited roaming with this thing!"

The next day at school, Sabrina tried to avoid Harvey, but she knew it would be impossible. Eventually she had to use her locker, and sure enough, he spotted her there. As he sauntered over, Sabrina twitched at the unusual awkwardness between them. "Hi," he said, rather tentatively.

"Hi."

"Listen, the other day when I said 'choose,'"

and he shrugged charmingly, "I meant 'choose *me.*'"

"I wish that was the *only* decision I had to make."

"What?"

"Nothing. Uh—have you gotten your mom a present yet?"

Shaking his head, Harvey confessed, "No. I still can't find anything perfect enough."

Despite the terrible decisions weighing on her mind, Sabrina felt good that she could at least help Harvey out of his fix. Softly she chanted,

> *"To get Harvey's mind off this romantic rift,*
> *send his mom the ideal gift."*

A *ping!* noise came from inside her locker. Trying to act casual, she opened the door to reveal a small, disgustingly cute—what Hilda would sarcastically call "precious"—porcelain figurine of an apple-cheeked little girl surrounded by big-eyed goats. "You're kidding," she muttered, a-mazed at some people's tastes. Carefully hefting the figurine, she held it up for Harvey to see. "How about this?"

To her shock, Harvey's eyes bugged in excitement. "Is that 'Heidi and Her Goat Friends'?"

"It . . . could be."

"My mom's been wanting it for years, but they stopped making it!"

"Three cheers for them."

Harvey didn't even hear her comment. He took the figurine and studied it with delight. "My mom'll pass out! How on earth did you ever get this?"

Sabrina couldn't resist. "Magic," she said.

Overwhelmed with gratitude, Harvey leaned over and kissed her cheek. Then, both tickled and embarrassed, he hurried away, tucking little Heidi and her goats carefully into his bookbag.

A little stunned, Sabrina closed her locker and headed for her first class, only to bump into Dashiell as she rounded a corner. He held out a bouquet. "Carrots," Sabrina noted, taking the bizarre bundle. "A little unusual, but thanks."

Dashiell grinned that cute grin of his. "They're not for you. I bought you a pony. Named Petey. So, do you like me better?"

Great. My choice of true love is devolving into a bribery contest. "Dash—" she began, but he ran over her protest.

"C'mon. There's an unimaginative mortal boy and me. What's your decision?"

"I'm thinking nunnery," she replied flatly, and walked off.

"Tick-tock. Clock's ticking." The Quizmaster now appeared among the jostling students in the hallway. Or had he been there the whole time?

"Your mom or your magic?" he demanded, as if expecting her answer then and there.

Sabrina was fed up. "Right now, magic," she said, and pointed, zapping the Quizmaster away. Pleased with her assertiveness, Sabrina started to walk again, only to hear the Quizmaster's bodiless voice following her.

"I can still do it from here," he said from . . . wherever he was. "Tick-tock, tick-tock!"

School was over, and Sabrina hurried home. Bookbag and carrots in hand, she entered the kitchen to find Mrs. Saberhagen cooking. "How would you like your salmon today, dear?"

"In huge portions?" replied Salem, who sat at the table with a napkin around his neck.

Sabrina held up her bouquet. "Anybody want carrots?"

"Tick-tock!" came the Quizmaster's voice.

Sabrina glared at the empty air. "Very subtle," she snapped.

Oblivious to all other concerns but her dear kitty-son, Mrs. Saberhagen reached for Sabrina's carrots. "I'll put some carrots in with the fish."

"No!" wailed Salem. "Don't taint it!"

Mrs. Saberhagen immediately backed away as if the carrots were diseased. "Whatever my puddin' cake wants," she cooed, and returned to her cooking.

Salem watched his mother, but he spoke to

Sabrina. "I can't believe I lived all those years without contact with my mom. I tell you, Sabrina, my heart is floating."

Sabrina's heart was doing anything but floating at the moment. "I gotta go think," she said, and turned to leave.

Just then, Mrs. Saberhagen sneezed. Sabrina considered fetching a tissue for her, but Salem beat her to it. "Are you catching a cold, Mummy? Here."

Mrs. Saberhagen took the tissue, dabbed her nose, and gazed lovingly at her son. He gazed back at her with his big golden eyes.

Sabrina fled up the stairs.

Once in her room, she flopped down onto her bed and moaned, "What am I going to do?" Hastily she added to the air, "I know, I know— *tick-tock.*"

It just wasn't fair. Seven days of bad luck had been rotten enough, and now this. It made the other days seem just inconvenient. Nobody really knew how much she missed her mom. Sure, she hid it most of the time. After all, what else could she do? The last thing she wanted was a ball of wax to call Mom. But at this point she was ready to give anything to see her mother again. Why did that "anything" have to be her magic?

She thought of Salem and his mother gazing at each other. "Salem . . ." said the image of Mrs. Saberhagen lovingly . . .

And her face blurred and melted and turned into Sabrina's own mother, the way she'd looked back when Sabrina was a little girl. "Sabrina . . ." her mother said to her lovingly. Little-girl Sabrina grinned to feel her mother's voice surround her like a warm, comforting blanket.

The daydream shattered and Sabrina sat up, tears stinging behind her eyes. "Oh, I miss my mom." She held up at her index finger and studied it. "But I love having magic." She thought of Heidi and her goat friends—she'd never have been able to please Harvey like that if she didn't have magic. And what about Valerie, who had been absolutely elated after Sabrina zapped a clothing tag to read "20% off" (even though Sabrina had to make up the difference later). She'd never be able to grant little favors like that anymore.

Sabrina stood up tall, her expression resolute. "I know what I have to do."

Downstairs in the kitchen, Salem had no idea what he was going to have to do in the next minute. His mother was still sneezing. "Maybe you put too much pepper in the peppers?" he suggested.

Mrs. Saberhagen sniffled. "The only time I sneezed this much—" *sneeze!* "—was two hundred years ago—" *sneeze!* "—when your father brought home that stray—" She stopped and met Salem's eyes.

"Cat," they both finished together, then she sneezed again.

Salem couldn't believe his rotten luck. His mother not only loved him enough to cater to his every whim, but she loved him as a cat and catered to his every cat whim! And now she was allergic to him! *"Nooooo!"* he howled in dismay.

Upstairs in her room, Sabrina could barely hear Salem's howl. What little of it that did reach her ears didn't register—she was too busy howling herself. "Quizmaster!"

He instantly appeared.

"I've made my decision."

"Good, because—" He gestured, and a loud alarm went off. When Sabrina failed to smile, the Quizmaster shrugged. "Sorry. I was just trying to lighten things up."

Sabrina made her announcement. "I love being a witch."

"So that's your decision?"

"But I can't go the rest of my life without seeing my mother." Clearly, *that* was her decision.

"You realize what this means," the Quizmaster said, all his joking aside. "Your powers will be gone forever. You won't even be able to do card tricks."

"This is the hardest decision I've ever had to make," Sabrina told him, "but I've made up my mind."

Reluctantly, the Quizmaster nodded. "All

right then." A cloth sack appeared in his hand. Holding it open, he gestured at Sabrina, and suddenly she felt a pull from deep within her, as if her soul were on the end of a string and somebody was trying to yank it out. It didn't so much hurt as feel strange, and it made her dizzy. Her right arm lifted up on its own, and her index finger pointed, shooting out a long comet's tail of sparkles—her magic! The Quizmaster was drawing the magic out of her! The trail of sparkles flew into the open sack, and when it was all over, Sabrina felt completely drained and the cloth sack was bulging.

She didn't even realize she was swaying on her feet until the Quizmaster held out a hand to steady her. "You okay?" he asked, his voice full of sympathy. "I've seen more color in plain yogurt."

Sabrina glanced in the mirror and realized he was right. She looked awful. Her face was pale, and her hair hung like limp spaghetti. All the sparkle was gone from her eyes. Even her clothes looked wrinkled . . . or maybe it was because she was slouching. "I feel nervous and insecure and self-conscious and extremely depressed," she muttered.

"Then the transformation is complete," the Quizmaster said, patting her shoulder. "You're a normal teenager again."

Sabrina couldn't laugh. She just asked, "Do me a favor? Zap me to my mom."

"Sure thing." The Quizmaster pointed.

A fraction of a second later, Sabrina fell rump-first onto the pebbly top of a mountain in Peru. "You could've been a little more gentle," she snapped in irritation.

The Quizmaster didn't answer. Instead, a familiar voice cried out, "Sabrina?"

Sabrina turned. "Mom!"

Sabrina and her mother rushed to greet each other. Her mother's warm embrace made Sabrina feel like a little girl again—safe and secure, the way she'd felt before all the witchy truths had turned her reality upside down. It felt so good!

Then her mother pulled away, looking startled. "Why aren't I a ball of wax?"

"Because," Sabrina announced, "I'm not a witch anymore."

Her mother's surprise turned to puzzlement. "What happened?"

"It's kind of a long story. Is there a dung hill where we can go sit and talk?"

In the Other Realm, Zelda was still rummaging through her mother's house. "There must be something of yours that Mother kept."

Hilda just stood in disgust, refusing to look any further. "Give it up, Zelda. There's nothing." She happened to glance down. "Wait a minute. I found something."

"What?" Zelda asked, excited.

"This stain on the rug. I spilled ink when I was young."

"That's right. Mother had just made friends with Rorschach."

Hilda gestured at the rug despondently. *"That* is how she remembers me. A smudge on the carpet of her life."

Zelda saw something else. "What's this?" From a table she picked up a small, crudely formed clay blob. Obviously it was supposed to be a sculpture, such as a child would make. Zelda read the note attached to it: "The first thing little Hilda ever zapped."

Hilda recognized the blob, and her despondency melted a bit. "My little clay horse!"

Zelda seemed surprised to learn that was what the blob was supposed to be. Looking at it with a fresh eye, she asked, "Why is it in pain?"

Hilda snatched it up. "Because I gave it corrective shoes," she snapped. "The point is, this stupid little thing meant so much to her, she kept it all these years." She paused thoughtfully. "She didn't keep anything like this of yours. Maybe she does like me best."

Zelda had an acid retort ready, but the phone rang, ruining the moment. Zelda plucked up the receiver. "Hello . . . ? Mother, where are you? Hilda and I have been waiting. . . ."

Curious, Hilda took a step forward, clutching her zap-sculpture.

"Oh. I see . . . Uh huh . . ." continued Zelda mysteriously. "All right, Mother. Good-bye." She hung up.

"What? What? What?"

"She's with Vesta. They went shopping. Vesta bought her some new ears. And now Vesta's taking her to the Riviera to show them off."

The two sisters stood staring at each other, realizing that they'd been waiting around all this time to see someone who'd had no intention of showing up. Instead, their beloved mother was off with their hyper-stylish, supermodel-ish, high-society, jet-setting sister, Vesta.

Hilda frowned. "I know she's our sister, and I love Vesta, but where does she get off living so long?"

Zelda shrugged. "But it does solve the mystery."

Hilda nodded. "Our mother's favorite daughter—"

They both sighed. "Vesta."

High atop a mountain in Peru, Sabrina and her mother sat around a camp fire with several Peruvian Indians, eating dinner from crude tin plates while various insectoid life forms buzzed around their heads.

One of the Indians turned politely to Sabrina, a pot and ladle poised in his hands. "More beetle puree?"

"No!" Sabrina said hastily, then added, "Thank you. But it was wonderful. Except for the taste."

Sabrina's mother gestured at their rugged surroundings. "The life of an archaeologist."

"Do you ever regret not staying an archaeology teacher and living a comfortable indoor life?" Sabrina asked her.

"There's no such thing as a perfect life," her mother answered. "Every choice we make has good parts and bad parts."

Sabrina's tongue felt something hard between her teeth. She pulled it out and grimaced at it. "Beetle husk."

Her mother gestured at it philosophically. "Bad part."

"I know what you mean. Giving up magic was bad, but then I got you. Of course, I'm risking malaria, but it was a lovely sunset. And I still don't know who to choose—Harvey or Dash."

"Here's what I'd do. Make a list of pros and cons for each guy. Then throw that list out and go with your heart."

Sabrina laughed. It was so nice to hear her mother's goofy jokes again. And her sound advice. "I miss you."

"I miss you, too." They hugged again, then her mother said, "So, any other questions only a mother can answer?"

"Yeah. How do I get down off this mountain?"

All too quickly, Sabrina got the answer to that

question. It wasn't exactly the answer she'd been expecting, but then again, this was Peru and her mother did live a rugged life. "Have a safe trip," her mother told her. "See you soon."

Sabrina shifted uncomfortably as her burro ambled forward at maybe one mile an hour. " 'Bye!" she said, then flicked the reins. The burro plodded a few more feet. " 'Bye!" *Plod plod.* " 'Bye!" *Plod plod plod.* "See you soon!" *Plod plod.* "Maybe you should call my aunts and tell them I might be late . . ."

Zelda entered the kitchen to find Salem hanging up the phone and crying. "Now why are you crying?" she asked him.

"My mom went to a doctor for allergy treatments," Salem blubbered. "She's going to take the needle just for me!"

Zelda gave the cat a reassuring pat. "I'm sorry you only got to see her for a short time."

As if a switch had been flicked, Salem straightened up, perfectly normal again. "She's my mother," he declared in a matter-of-fact tone. "A short time's plenty."

"Look what I found!" Hilda entered with Sabrina, her face smeared with dirt, her clothes coated with grime, and her whole body registering utter exhaustion. Hilda thought a positive identification might be necessary, so she added, "It's Sabrina!"

Zelda helped Sabrina to a chair. "Are you all right?"

"I rode a burro to a truck, a truck to a bus, and the bus to an airplane." Sabrina winced at the memories. "The burro was the best part." She was so tired she didn't even react when her Quizmaster appeared.

"How was the trip to Peru?" he asked. "I meant to ask you to pick me up an alpaca sweater."

She gave him a baleful look. "Why are you here? I don't need a quizmaster anymore."

"Soap is what she needs," Hilda said. "And a wire brush."

The Quizmaster ignored the aunts and zeroed in on Sabrina. "I know you're going to get mad when you hear this but," he paused, "this whole thing was a test."

Sabrina felt as if he'd just smacked her upside the head. *"What?"*

"Maybe I should've broken the news away from all these sharp objects."

"What kind of test? What are you talking about?" Sabrina lunged to her feet, filled with sudden energy, and turned to her aunts. "Why is he always doing this to me?" There was nothing they could say, so Sabrina decided to take revenge. In vain she tried to swing her leg, but she couldn't do it. "My clothes are too encrusted with dirt! Wouldn't someone please kick him?"

Realizing he was in hot water, the Quizmaster held up his hands in the universal "Don't hit me" pose. "One of the most important tests you have to take before getting your witch's license—maybe the *most* important—is to show that there is something in this universe that means more to you than magic," he explained.

"And you proved it by choosing your mother," Hilda added.

"And we couldn't be prouder of you," Zelda finished earnestly.

"Let me guess," Sabrina glared at her aunts. "You two were in on this?"

Zelda nodded. "We had to leave you alone so you could pass the test by yourself."

"Although why we couldn't have just gone to Acapulco still baffles me," said Hilda.

The whole thing still didn't make sense to Sabrina. "But it couldn't have only been a test. What about the mirror? My week of—" she stopped herself. "Horrible luck? My powers were really gone. That's why I had to ride four hundred miles in a truck full of chickens."

"The mirror was real. You survived every temptation the week sent you. Seemed like good cramming for the final." He smiled. "Your powers were taken away so you could visit your mother, and now that you're back, so is your magic." The cloth sack holding Sabrina's magic appeared in his hands, and with a flourish, he opened it up. A tide of sparkles burst out and zipped into Sabrina's pointing fingertip like they were being sucked up into a straw.

Sabrina shivered. It was like drinking six glasses of sugar soda in a row—every fiber of her being felt totally energized all at once. She was still a teenager with typical teenager problems, but now she felt hope. With magic, anything was possible!

Holding up her finger, Sabrina grinned. "So I can really zap again?"

"Absolutely."

"Then what am I waiting for?" With ruthless pleasure, Sabrina pointed at the Quizmaster. *Zap!*

A thousand miles away on a poultry truck bouncing across the Peruvian wilderness, the Quizmaster found himself surrounded by chickens—cages and cages and cages full of clucking, pecking chickens. "This is a thankless job," he sighed.

Later that night, Sabrina's aunts badgered her about the one important decision that she hadn't yet made. "What about Harvey and Dashiell?" Zelda asked.

"Yeah," said Hilda. "Who are you going to choose? We're dying to know."

Sabrina was heading for her room, her aunts trailing after her like a couple of groupies. "My mom said to follow my heart, so that's what I'm going to do," Sabrina told them.

"That's how I ended up sharing a studio apartment with Vlad the Impaler," warned Hilda.

As usual, Zelda ignored her sister. "So who are you going to pick?"

"I don't know. I guess I have time to decide—"

"Tick-tock!" came the Quizmaster's bodiless voice.

Sabrina reached her room. "Quit it!" she yelled at him, and closed the door.

Outside, Hilda sniffed and called, "Is there an E.T.A. on that bath?"

An hour later, Sabrina still hadn't taken her bath. She paced back and forth in the room, still dressed in her filthy clothes. "Dash is really sweet and funny, but Harvey's really sweet and funny," she said aloud, struggling with her decision. "But Dash is half-witch, so we have so much in common. But Harvey and I have so much history together. Dash has that great smile. But Harvey has those puppy-dog eyes. I don't have to hide my magic around Dash. But nobody knows me like Harvey." She stopped pacing. "You know what I don't like about them, though? They're putting me through this. I don't know how I'm ever going to decide. What do you think?"

"I *could* tell you matters of the heart take time. That you can't solve this right now." Salem sat on her bed with a clothespin on his nose. "But I *do* think you smell," he said, his voice squeaky because his nose was pinned. "Could we at least run a bath while you talk?"

Sabrina gestured at the burro—a gift from the Quizmaster. "I really don't think it's me, Salem."

Salem glared at the burro. "Good grief, man, be civilized! Some of us use a box."

And over in the corner of the room, the magic mirror sighed as her last piece floated into place. She had her center. She was complete.

"Of course Sabrina was going to pass the test. The answer was right in front of my nose."

Right in front of her nose was Sabrina, a true witch.

About the Authors

About the Authors

Nancy Holder has written thirty-six books and over two hundred short stories, game fiction, and comic books and TV commercials in Japan. Her books include *Buffy the Vampire Slayer: The Angel Chronicles, Volume 1.* She and her writing partner, Christopher Golden, have also written several other *Buffy* books, including *The Watcher's Guide,* the official companion guide to the show. Her next *Sabrina* novel, *Scarabian Nights,* will be available this summer. She lives in San Diego with her husband, Wayne, and their daughter, Belle.

Diana G. Gallagher is a Hugo Award–winning artist, best known for her series *Woof: The House Dragon.* Her first adult novel, *The Alien Dark,* appeared in 1990. She co-authored *The Chance Factor,* a *Star Trek: Starfleet Academy: Voyager* book, with her husband, Martin R. Burke. In addition to other *Star Trek* novels for intermediate readers, Diana has written many books in series published by Minstrel Books, including *The Secret World of Alex Mack, Are You Afraid of the Dark?* and *The Mystery Files of Shelby Woo*. She is currently working on original young adult novels for the Archway paperback series *Sabrina, the Teenage Witch*.

Ray Garton is author of several young adult books, including three *Sabrina* books—*Ben There, Done That* and the young reader novelization *The Troll Bride* (both as Joseph Locke), and *All That Glitters*. He does extensive research for each of his *Sabrina, the Teenage Witch* novels. His hobbies include invisibility, levitation, time travel, and turning children into hermit crabs.

Author of two *Sabrina* novels and the novelization for *Sabrina Goes to Rome*, **Mel Odom** is happily engaged in making magic. His daughter Montana first got him interested in *Sabrina, the Teenage Witch*, but he's since developed a fascination with Salem, because the talking cat reminds Mel of a lot of the friends he himself had back in high school—the ones his parents told him to stay away from. Thankfully, those same friends influenced him and got him in enough trouble—er, kept him artistically inclined enough—that it's no problem to think of new crises to put Sabrina and her friends through. He also loves E-mail correspondence and can be reached at denimbyte@aol.com.

Mark Dubowski has written and illustrated many books. His first professional writing job was to come up with an advertisement for a gingerbread cookie. When he finished, he got to eat the cookie!

Cathy East Dubowski's favorite Christmas story is *A Christmas Carol* by Charles Dickens, so she had lots of fun combining it with the magic of a Sabrina story. Cathy writes in an old red barn in North Carolina, where she lives with her husband and sometimes collaborator, Mark Dubowski, her daughters, Lauren and Megan, and their golden retriever, Macdougal. [Psst! If you know *A Christmas Carol* only from having seen the cartoon versions of it, Cathy suggests you read the original Dickens book as soon as possible! It's very short, very funny, and very scary!]

David Cody Weiss and **Bobbi JG Weiss** are actually witches from the Other Realm. So amused are they by Sabrina's antics that they've decided to write for the book series, thereby making sure that all magical spells mentioned in the stories are current and that all witch facts are correct. David and Bobbi share their abode with five talking witch cats named Ditto, Newt, Little Molly Tubguts, Bumpus, and Buzzboy. When everyone talks at once, it's a real mess!

Win a trip to Hollywood!

to record your own CD in celebration
of the official Sabrina soundtrack in the
"SABRINA SING-A-LONG SWEEPSTAKES!"

MUSIC FROM **SABRINA, THE TEENAGE WITCH** ON GEFFEN RECORDS

1 GRAND PRIZE

A trip for two (winner and chaperone) to Hollywood for a recording session sponsored by Geffen Records, Inc. Winner will also receive 25 copies of their recorded CD, a visit to the Sabrina, The Teenage Witch™ set at Paramount Pictures, and a "Sabrina, The Teenage Witch" licensed merchandise package.

☆ See next page for exciting runner-up prizes! ☆

Complete entry form and send to:
Pocket Books/"Sabrina Sing-A-Long Sweepstakes"
13th Floor, 1230 Avenue of the Americas, NY, NY 10020

Name_____Birthdate____/____/_____

Address_____

City_____State/Province_____

Zip code/PC_____Phone (____) _____

5 FIRST PRIZES

A magical "Sabrina, The Teenage Witch" gift package featuring Archway Paperbacks' Sabrina, The Teenage Witch: Magic Handbook, Tiger Electronics' crystal ball and psychic telephone, Pastime Industries' craft kits, Geffen Records' "Sabrina, The Teenage Witch" soundtrack CD, and make-up from Cosrich all packed in a Honey Fashions "Sabrina, The Teenage Witch" backpack

10 SECOND PRIZES

A complete set of "Sabrina, The Teenage Witch" books from Archway Paperbacks published by Pocket Books and a "Sabrina, The Teenage Witch" soundtrack CD from Geffen Records, Inc.

15 THIRD PRIZES

A "Sabrina, The Teenage Witch" psychic telephone and crystal ball from Tiger Electronics and a "Sabrina, The Teenage Witch" soundtrack CD from Geffen Records, Inc.

25 FOURTH PRIZES

A "Sabrina, The Teenage Witch: Spellbound" CD-Rom adventure game from Simon & Schuster Interactive/Knowledge Adventure, Inc. and a "Sabrina, The Teenage Witch" soundtrack CD from Geffen Records, Inc.

50 FIFTH PRIZES

A one year "Sabrina, The Teenage Witch" subscription from Archie Comics and a "Sabrina, The Teenage Witch" soundtrack CD from Geffen Records, Inc.

100 SIXTH PRIZES

A "Sabrina, The Teenage Witch" soundtrack CD from Geffen Records, Inc.

TIGER ELECTRONICS INC.

Paramount

Knowledge Adventure

VIACOM

SIMON & SCHUSTER

Pastime

Archie

See next page for official rules 2015 (2of3)

Pocket Books/ "Sabrina Sing-A-Long Sweepstakes"Sponsors Official Rules:

1. No Purchase Necessary. Enter by mailing this completed Official Entry Form (no copies allowed) or by mailing a 3" x 5" card with your name and address, daytime telephone number and birthdate to the Pocket Books/ "Sabrina Sing-A-Long Sweepstakes", 1230 Avenue of the Americas, 13th Floor, NY, NY 10020. Entry forms are available in the back of Archway Paperbacks' Sabrina, The Teenage Witch: SABRINA GOES TO ROME and HARVEST MOON by Mel Odom and NOW YOU SEE HER , NOW YOU DON'T by Diana Gallagher, on in-store book displays, on the web site SimonSays.com and on coupons inside Geffen Records' CDs. Sweepstakes begins 9/8/98. Entries must be received by 12/31/98. Not responsible for lost, late, damaged, stolen, illegible, mutilated, incomplete, or misdirected or not delivered entries or mail or for typographical errors in the entry form or rules. Entries are void if they are in whole or in part illegible, incomplete or damaged. Enter as often as you wish, but each entry must be mailed separately. Winners will be selected at random from all eligible entries received in a drawing to be held on or about 2/1/99. Winners must be available to travel during the months of February and March1999. Winners will be notified by mail.

2. Prizes: One Grand Prize: A 3-day/2-night stay for two (winner and chaperone, chaperone must be winner's parent or legal guardian) to Hollywood including round-trip coach airfare from major U.S. airport nearest the winner's residence, round-trip transportation to and from airport, hotel accommodations and all meals. Winner will also receive a recording session sponsored by Geffen Records, Inc. 25 copies of their recorded CD, a visit to the "Sabrina, The Teenage Witch" set at Paramount Pictures, a "Sabrina, The Teenage Witch" gift package (from Archway Paperbacks, Cosrich, Geffen Records, Inc. Simon & Schuster Interactive/Knowledge Adventure, Inc. and Tiger Electronics (approx. retail value: $2,500). Five First Prizes: A magical "Sabrina, The Teenage Witch" gift package with Archway Paperbacks' Sabrina, The Teenage Witch: Magic Handbook, Tiger Electronics' psychic telephone and crystal ball, Pastime Industries' craft kits, Geffen Records' "Sabrina, The Teenage Witch" soundtrack CD, and make-up from Cosrich all packed in a Honey Fashions "Sabrina, The Teenage Witch" backpack (approx. retail value: $120.00). Ten Second Prizes: A complete set of "Sabrina, The Teenage Witch" books from Archway Paperbacks published by Pocket Books and a "Sabrina, The Teenage Witch" soundtrack CD from Geffen Records, Inc. (approx. retail value: $95.00). Fifteen Third Prizes: a "Sabrina, The Teenage Witch" psychic telephone and crystal ball from Tiger Electronics and a "Sabrina, The Teenage Witch" soundtrack CD from Geffen Records, Inc. (approx. retail value: $70.00). Twenty-Five Fourth Prizes: A "Sabrina, The Teenage Witch: Spellbound" CD-Rom adventure game from SSI/Knowledge Adventure, Inc. and a "Sabrina, The Teenage Witch" soundtrack CD from Geffen Records, Inc. (approx. retail value: $45.00). Fifty Fifth Prizes: a one year subscription to "Sabrina, The Teenage Witch" comics from Archie Comics and a "Sabrina, The Teenage Witch" soundtrack CD from Geffen Records, Inc. (approx. retail value: $35.00). One Hundred Sixth Prizes: a "Sabrina, The Teenage Witch" soundtrack CD from Geffen Records, Inc. (approx. retail value: $15.00). The Grand Prize must be taken on the date specified by sponsors.

3. The sweepstakes is open to legal residents of the U.S. and Canada (excluding Quebec) ages 8-15 as of 12/31/98, except as set forth below. Proof of age is required to claim prize. Prizes will be awarded to the winner's parent or legal guardian. Void in Puerto Rico and wherever prohibited or restricted by law. All federal, state and local laws apply. Viacom International, Inc. Archie Comic Publications Inc., Geffen Records, Inc. and Universal Music and Video Distribution, Inc. their respective officers, directors, shareholders, employees, parent, subsidiaries, affiliates, agencies, sponsors, participating retailers, and persons connected with the use, marketing or conduct of this sweepstakes are not eligible. Family members living in the same household as any of the individuals referred to in the preceding sentence are not eligible.

4. One prize per person or household. Prizes are not transferable and may not be substituted except by sponsors, in the event of prize unavailability, in which case a prize of equal or greater value will be awarded. Prizes are subject to production schedule and availability of talent. All prizes will be awarded. The odds of winning a prize depend upon the number of eligible entries received.

5.If a winner is a Canadian resident, then he/she must correctly answer a skill-based question administered by mail.

6. All expenses on receipt and use of prize including federal, state and local taxes are the sole responsibility of the winners. Winners will be notified by mail. Winners may be required to execute and return an Affidavit of Eligibility and Release and all other legal documents which the sweepstakes sponsor may require (including a W-9 tax form) within 15 days of attempted notification or an alternate winner will be selected. The Grand Prize Winner's travel companion will be required to execute a liability release form prior to ticketing.

7. Winners or winners' parents on winners' behalf agree to allow use of their names, photographs, likenesses, and entries for any advertising, promotion and publicity purposes without further compensation to or permission from the entrants, except where prohibited by law.

8. Winners agree that Viacom International, Inc., Archie Comic Publications Inc. and Geffen Records, Inc. and their respective officers, directors, shareholders, employees, suppliers, parent, subsidiaries, affiliates, agencies, sponsors, participating retailers, and persons connected with the use, marketing or conduct of this sweepstakes, shall have no responsibility or liability for injuries, losses or damages of any kind in connection with the collection, acceptance or use of the prizes awarded herein, or from participation in this promotion.

9. By participating in this sweepstakes, entrants agree to be bound by these rules and the decisions of the judges and sweepstakes sponsors, which are final in all matters relating to the sweepstakes. Failure to comply with the Official Rules may result in a disqualification of your entry and prohibition of any further participation in these sweepstakes.

10. The names the of major winners will be posted at SimonSays.com (available after 2/1/99) or the names of the winners may be obtained by sending a stamped, self-addressed envelope to Prize Winners, Pocket Books "Sabrina Sing-A-Long Sweepstakes," 1230 Avenue of the Americas, 13th Floor, NY, NY 10020.

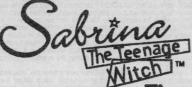